THE GUNSMITH

#29

WILDCAT ROUNDUP

Other Books
By
J.R. Roberts

Macklin's Women
The Chinese Gunmen
The Woman Hunt
The Guns of Abilene
Three Guns for Glory
Leadtown
The Longhorn War
Quanah's Revenge
Heavyweight Gun
New Orleans Fire
One-Handed Gun
The Canadian Payroll
Draw to an Inside Death
Dead Man's Hand
Bandit Gold
Buckskins and Six-Guns
Silver War
High Noon at Lancaster
Bandido Blood
The Dodge City Gang
Sasquatch Hunt
Bullets and Ballots
The Riverboat Gang
Killer Grizzly
North of the Border
Eagle's Gap

Chinatown Hell
The Panhandle Search
Wildcat Roundup
The Ponderosa War
Trouble Rides a Fast Horse
Dynamite Justice
The Posse
Night of the Gila
The Bounty Women
Black Pearl Saloon
Gundown in Paradise
King of the Border
The El Paso Salt War
The Ten Pines Killer
Hell with a Pistol
Wyoming Cattle Kill
The Golden Horseman
The Scarlet Gun
Navaho Devil
Wild Bill's Ghost
The Miner's Showdown
Archer's Revenge
Showdown in Raton
When Legends Meet
Desert Hell
The Diamond Gun

For more exciting
E-Books, Audiobooks and MP3 downloads visit us at
www.speakingvolumes.us

THE GUNSMITH

#29

WILDCAT ROUNDUP

J.R. ROBERTS

SPEAKING VOLUMES, LLC
NAPLES, FLORIDA
2013

THE GUNSMITH
#29 WILDCAT ROUNDUP

ISBN 978-1-61232-632-0

To Dirty Gordy

Chapter One

Clint Adams could feel the tension in the air the moment he entered the room. As he approached the bar, the saloon fell deathly silent—the kind of silence that is usually followed by death, that is. He wanted to turn around and walk right out again, but he had been traveling a long time; he had hoped to get a room, and some cold beer, and rest up before continuing. He squared his shoulders and leaned against the bar.

"Beer," he said to the barkeep.

"Sure," the man said nervously. He was a small man in his late forties, and his hand shook as he placed a mug of cold beer in front of Clint.

"Is it always this quiet?" Clint asked.

"I, ah, don't know," the man replied.

"You don't know?"

"I, uh, got to wipe the other end of the bar," the bartender said, and hurried away with a damp, dirty rag. At the other end he began to rub frantically at the bar top, keeping his eyes glued to the rag.

"Shit," Clint said, under his breath.

He had ridden into the town of Voluntario, Texas, on the Mexican border, tired, thirsty, and hungry. After putting his rig and horse, Duke, up in the livery, he had registered in the hotel and come to the saloon for a cold beer. Next on his agenda was a hot meal, but he had the feeling now that that would not be so easy.

1

He sipped his beer and kept his eyes on the mirror behind the bar. The saloon was about half full at midday, and it was still quiet.

The clerk in the hotel had recognized him immediately, he knew, even before he'd signed the register. In the past his name had cost him more trouble than a man's name should, yet he could never bring himself to deny it. He studied the faces of the men behind him and wondered which of them it would be. Would he be able to finish his beer before he was forced to kill someone?

How could one man force another to kill? he thought. It will happen only if I let it.

He put the beer down, half finished, and turned to leave the saloon, instinctively knowing that he would not make it, but ready to try anyway.

He was halfway to the door before the man spoke up.

"Leaving already? You didn't finish your beer."

Adams turned his head and located the speaker. He wasn't even a full-grown man, just a boy of about eighteen or so. The gun on his hip, however, would be just as deadly in his hand as in the hand of a man thirty or forty.

"I'm not thirsty anymore," he said.

"Or maybe you're just scared," the boy suggested.

"Of what?" Clint asked. "A pup with a gun? Be careful you don't shoot off your foot, sonny."

Immediately, he cursed himself for having said the wrong thing. Instead of making the kid back down, he had gotten the kid's back up. He could see it in the boy's eyes, the bloodlust, the urge to kill, or get killed.

"I'm walking out of here, boy," Clint said. There was nothing he could say now that would appease the boy, so he didn't try to talk him out of anything. He just said, "If you try and stop me, you'll make me kill you, and I don't want to do that."

"The Gunsmith," the boy said, contemptuously, "afraid

of a 'boy' with a gun, huh? Everybody here is gonna say it was that way, mister."

"Everybody here can say what they want," Clint replied. "The same won't be true for you if you don't back away, boy."

"I can take you," the boy said.

"Cal—" a man who had been seated with the boy started to say, reaching a hand out to him, but the boy pulled his arm away.

"You related to him, mister?" Clint asked.

"He's my cousin," the man replied. He was about six or seven years older than the boy.

"You're older than he is," Clint said. "Maybe you're smarter, too. Talk some sense into him. All I want is a hot meal and a place to sleep. I'll be on my way in the morning. Keep him out of my way until then."

"I'll try—" the man started, but the boy didn't let him finish.

"You'll try nothing," he said to his cousin. "You better back my play, Ray."

"Cal," the man named Ray said, "that there's the Gunsmith, but he don't want no trouble."

"He's yella," the boy said, still keeping his eyes on the Gunsmith.

"No he ain't, Cal," Ray insisted. "Look at him, boy, goddamn it!" the other man said, suddenly agitated. "Don't go gettin' yourself killed for nothing."

Now the boy called Cal looked at his cousin and said, "You're yella, too."

He turned his eyes back to the Gunsmith, and his cousin stood up quickly and swung his right hand. His fist exploded against the boy's cheek, knocking him to the ground. He tried to get up but his cousin, the bigger of the two, put his foot on his chest and pushed him back down.

He looked at the Gunsmith and said, "You better leave,

4

mister. I thank you for not killing him."

Clint looked down at the boy, who was glaring first at him and then at his cousin with the same hatred on his face, and thought that it still might happen, but he didn't say as much.

"Just keep a short tether on him, Ray," he said. "I'll be gone by morning."

"Don't worry," Ray said.

"Much obliged," Clint said, and walked out of the saloon.

He went in search of a café or restaurant, all the while thinking maybe he should just leave town, but the weariness he felt in his bones and the hunger in his belly wouldn't let him do that.

He'd succeeded in avoiding killing the boy, Cal, so maybe that would be the end of it. Maybe his cousin Ray would talk the kid out of trying it again.

Yeah, and maybe the sun wouldn't come up in the morning.

As Raphael Ramirez rode into Voluntario with his two colleagues he hoped that this would be the end of their search. He longed to get back to his native South America which, even with the problem of the Devil Cat, seemed almost tame compared to America's "Wild West." He had always thought that term to be the product of the writers of cheap fiction, but in the short weeks he had been in this country, he had seen men beaten and shot for nothing more than a drink, or an inadvertent jostling on the street.

Barbaric.

"Ernesto," he said to the younger man on his right, "you take the horses to the stable, your brother and I will register at the hotel."

"*Si*, Uncle," Ernesto said.

"Uncle?" the other man said as they were dismounting.

"Yes, Eduardo?" the old man said, groaning with the

effort dismounting caused his fifty-five-year-old body.

"Do you think he will be here?"

"I do not know, Eduardo," Ramirez replied. "Ernesto, take the horses."

"Yes, Uncle."

"Come, Eduardo," Ramirez said, "we will register."

"I hope he is here," the younger man said as they entered the hotel lobby.

"As do I, nephew," the older man agreed. "If we do not find him here, I fear we will have to return without him."

"But the Devil Cat," the younger man complained.

"We will have to try again ourselves, Nesto," Ramirez said.

"But Uncle," Ernesto said, "he is the only man who can help us. The Gunsmith is the only man who can kill the Devil Cat for us." The young man took hold of his uncle's arm and said, "We must find the Gunsmith."

"Perhaps we will, Nesto," Raphael Ramirez said. "Perhaps here we will."

Chapter Two

When Clint left the café he was feeling better. He was no longer hungry, and he'd had two pots of strong, black coffee with dinner. He had all but forgotten the incident in the saloon, and was feeling fairly mellow, and not a little sleepy. He decided to go to his hotel room for at least a couple of hours sleep. After that he'd decide whether he should continue sleeping, or go looking for either a poker game, or a woman.

As he stepped into the street, however, the decision was taken out of his hands.

"Hey, Gunsmith," a voice called. He turned his head to the right and saw the kid, Cal, standing in the street, legs apart, hands at his side.

"Kid—"

"There's nobody here to stop us, Gunsmith," the kid said. "My cousin Ray, he sorta took an unscheduled nap."

The kid had cold-cocked his cousin so that he could brace Clint without any interference.

People on the streets began to take notice and stopped to watch. A young man, on his way to the hotel from the livery stable, also stopped, watching with interest.

"Cal, this is a mistake," Clint argued.

"You made the mistake, when you tried to make a fool of me in the saloon."

"I was trying to save your life."

"You were trying to save your own, by making a fool out of me," Cal said. "I can take you, Adams, and I think you know it."

"Fine," Clint said, "then let's leave it at that."

"Oh, no," Cal said. "I want them to know it, too," he said, pointing to the spectators who now lined the street. They had heard Cal call Clint "the Gunsmith" and many of them knew the name well.

"There's only one way you're going to get off this street, Adams," the kid said, "and that's feet first."

"Son," Clint said, turning to face the kid squarely, "you're digging your own grave."

"I'll tell you what, Gunsmith," Cal said. "When this is all over, I'll do you a favor and dig yours. That's the best offer you're gonna get."

There was about twenty feet separating them, and Clint started to take a step towards the kid.

"This is close enough, Adams," the kid said, "or do you need to be closer? Afraid you'll miss? Don't worry about that. You won't even clear leather—" Cal said, and then his hand streaked for his gun.

To Clint Adams, the kid's hand was moving in slow motion. He had grossly overrated his chances against the Gunsmith.

Clint slid his gun smoothly from his holster and fired a shot at the kid. His bullet followed an unerring path, but as Cal went for his gun he crouched down and leaned to his left. It was a move designed to aid his chances, but in this case it negated them. The bullet, which had been meant for his shoulder, caught him in the throat, just beneath the chin. The force of the impact threw his head back, and he toppled over backward, gagging on the torrent of blood that welled up in his throat.

"Shit," Clint said, immediately realizing that the kid had

as good as killed himself twice—by calling him out in the first place and then by moving as Clint had fired.

Holstering his gun he covered the twenty feet between them as quickly as possible, but by the time he reached the fallen man, it was too late. The kid was dead.

"I saw him, Uncle."

"Calm down, Eduardo," Ramirez said. His nephew had come bursting into the room, out of breath from running, and insisting that he had found the Gunsmith.

"Does this have something to do with the shot we heard?" Ramirez asked.

"Yes, it was him," Eduardo said, excitedly. "The stories are true, Nesto," he added to his brother.

"What stories?" Ramirez demanded.

"The stories we have heard of this man since our arrival in this country," Ernesto explained.

"About his hunting prowess?" the older man asked.

"About his speed with a gun," Eduardo said.

"You have heard these stories and have not told me?" Ramirez demanded.

"We knew you did not want to hire a gunman, Uncle," Eduardo said, "but a hunter."

"And this man is both," Ernesto added. "Is he truly as fast as we have heard?" he asked his brother.

"Like the wind," Eduardo said. "Like the blink of an eye, like—"

"Enough," Ramirez said, and both young men fell silent. "How do you know it was him?"

"The other man called him 'the Gunsmith,' " Eduardo replied.

Ramirez thought a moment, then nodded. "We must talk with him, then," he said, finally, rising from his chair.

Both of his nephews stood up and hurried for the door.

"Wait," he called, and they stopped. "Where are you both going?"

"To talk to the Gunsmith," Ernest said.

"I am the emissary," their uncle reminded them. "I speak for the others."

They both looked chagrined and lowered their heads. Ernesto said, "Yes, Uncle."

Ramirez approached them then, touched them both on the shoulder affectionately. "Besides, where would you go to talk to him?"

Ernesto and Eduardo looked at each other, and then looked at their uncle rather sheepishly.

"We do not know," Ernesto, ever the spokesman for the two, said.

"Well, you are both lucky that I do," Ramirez said, picking up his hat.

"Where?"

"If he has just killed a man," Raphael Ramirez said, "then we will no doubt find him at the sheriff's office. Make sure the door is locked behind us, Ernesto."

Ernesto exchanged glances with his brother, and then said, "Yes, Uncle."

Chapter Three

"Why didn't you check in with me when you hit town?" the sheriff demanded of the Gunsmith.

"Sheriff, that's a habit of mine I rarely break," Clint told him, "but I just never did get the chance."

"Yeah," the sheriff said, rubbing his stomach. It always acted up after somebody got killed. Sheriff Willard Forbes suspected that the only killing that wouldn't leave him with an upset stomach would be his own.

"All right," Forbes said, "pick up your gun. Your story checks out."

"Thanks, Sheriff," Clint said. He stepped forward and picked up his gunbelt from the man's desk. Forbes was a tall man who had developed a roundness to his belly right about his fortieth birthday, and each year since then it had gotten bigger. In a couple of years, Clint guessed, the sheriff would be fifty or so, and would be having a hard time standing up from behind his desk. At that moment, the man lowered his bulk onto his chair with a groan.

"You plan on killin' anyone else while you're in town?" he asked, rubbing his belly absently with his left hand.

"That's not fair, Sheriff," Clint said, buckling his gunbelt, "I didn't plan on killing that boy."

"Maybe not," Forbes said, "but men like you always end up killing somebody, anyway."

"I'll be leaving in the morning, Sheriff," Clint said, "so you won't have anything to worry about."

11

"That suits me," Forbes said.

"Me, too," Clint said. He didn't relish staying in this town much longer, anyway. He knew the looks he'd be getting until he left in the morning. It was almost enough to make him leave right away, except that it would be dark in a couple of hours.

As he stepped out of the sheriff's office he saw three men approaching. The man in the middle was older, almost sixty, with the white hair that went with the age. The men flanking him were in their early twenties, and from where Clint stood they looked to be identical. As they got closer, he realized that they were.

"I'm seeing double," he said as the three men reached him.

"My nephews are twins," the older man said.

"I can see that."

"You are Clint Adams," the older man asked, "the one they call the Gunsmith?"

Clint sobered and said, "I'm Adams."

"My name is Raphael Ramirez, Mr. Adams," the man said, "and I have come a very long way to hire you."

"Mexico isn't so far away, Señor Ramirez."

"I did not come from Mexico," the man said. "I came from South America."

"South America?" Clint repeated. "Now, that is a long way."

"To be precise, my home is Paraguay."

"To be precise," Clint repeated, "what is this about wanting to hire me?"

"Can we go someplace and discuss it?" the man asked.

Clint looked at the two younger men and then asked, "All of us?"

The two nephews looked at their uncle anxiously, and the old man said, "If you do not mind."

"Hell, I don't mind," Clint said, "as long as you're buying while we're talking."

"If you mean whiskey," Ramirez said, "I am buying."

"I mean beer," Clint said. "That'll do for now."

Moments later they were seated at a back table with four mugs of beer in front of them. Clint had insisted on sitting with his back to the wall, and the other three had agreed without question. Oh, the nephews had questions, all right, but one look from their uncle had kept them from asking.

"Okay, you bought," Clint said, holding his beer, "now you can talk."

"We want—" Eduardo started quickly, but another look from his uncle silenced him. "Sorry, Uncle."

"We wish to hire you as a hunter," Ramirez told Clint.

"Of what?" Clint asked, suspiciously.

"The Devil Cat," Ernesto said, so quickly it was out before he even realized it.

"Nesto . . ." his uncle said, and Ernesto fell silent.

"What's this devil cat?"

"That is what our people call him," Ramirez said. "El Gato Diablo."

"What is he, mountain lion? Cougar?"

"Worse," Ramirez said, and his eyes sort of went out of focus, as if he were picturing the animal in his mind. "He is a jaguar, and he has the devil in his heart."

"He has no heart," Ernesto said, and his uncle did not chastize him this time.

"My nephew is right, of course," Ramirez said. "Mr. Adams, I am Raphael Ramirez, and these are my nephews, Ernesto and Eduardo. We are here representing many others who have ranches, who have been victimized."

"By the Devil Cat?"

"Yes."

"Why did they send you?"

"I was not sent," Ramirez said, stiff-backed. "I chose to come."

"Okay," Clint said with a shrug. "Why you?"

"I have been the most victimized."

"Have you lost the most cattle?"

Ramirez looked Clint straight in the eye and said, "I lost my only son."

Clint took a long, slow sip of his beer, and then carefully put the mug down on the table.

"And you want to hire me to kill this animal for you?" he asked.

"Yes," Ramirez said. "We have heard stories, about a great bear, and about sasquatch."

"You know the story of sasquatch?"

"Yes," Ramirez said, "his and yours."

"You think you know my story, huh?" Clint asked.

"We wish to hire you, Mr. Adams," Ramirez said. "There are many of us. We will pool our finances and pay you very well."

Clint picked up his beer, drained it, and put the empty mug down. "Not interested," he said, and stood up.

"What—" Ernesto said.

"But—" Eduardo chimed in.

Another look from their uncle quieted both of the twins.

"If you change your mind," Ramirez said, "we will be at the hotel. In the morning, we will be going back home."

"I'll be leaving in the morning too, Ramirez," Clint said. "I wish you and your people luck."

Clint turned and left the saloon, heading back to the hotel. He'd had his fill of animals with the devil where their heart ought to be. Ole Three Paw* had been like that, and the Sasquatch.** What he didn't need to do was tangle with

*The Gunsmith #24: Killer Grizzly
**The Gunsmith #21: Sasquatch Hunt

some South American cat that was worse than a mountain lion.

When he got to the hotel all he was thinking about was a good night's sleep, and an early start, but that wasn't to be.

When he entered the hotel lobby there were three or four men waiting there for him. They were all armed . . . with pencils.

"Mr. Adams," they all called, advancing on him at once.

"What's going on here?" he demanded.

"We'd like to get a story from you, Mr. Adams," one man said.

"A story about what?"

"We'd like to know what the Gunsmith is doing in this part of the country," one man asked.

"That man you killed today," another man said, "how many does that make?"

Clint pinned the man's ears back with a glare, and then asked, "Are you all newspapermen?"

"That's right," one said.

"I've got nothing to say to any of you," he said, and headed for the stairs.

"It's not that easy, Adams," one of them called out. "You're big news. By tomorrow, there'll be other newspapermen here too," the man told him.

"You'd do well to talk to us now," another man said.

"I won't be talking to any newspapermen," Clint said to them all. Damn it, he thought, it was a newspaperman who christened him the Gunsmith more than twenty years ago. He had no liking for them, in general.

"You'd have to leave the area in a pretty big hurry to avoid us, and the rest," a man said to him.

"Is that a fact?" Clint asked. "I'll bet there's one of you fellas hidden under my bed upstairs."

"I wouldn't put it past someone," a voice called out.

"No," Clint said, "neither would I. Only thing is, if I find one of you in my room, he's going to leave the hard way . . . through the window!''

As one, the newsmen took a couple of steps backward, and Clint called out, ''Just keep moving back, Gents, until you're all out the door, unless you want me to be tempted to shoot a few ears off.''

''You wouldn't,'' one of them said.

''Why not? Isn't that one of the things men like me are supposed to do?'' he demanded.

By the time the question was out of his mouth, there was no one left to answer it.

With the newspapermen gone, Clint walked up to the desk clerk and said, ''You have a Ramirez registered here?''

''Yes, sir,'' the frightened desk clerk said. ''Three of them.''

''Give them a message for me, will you?''

''Y-yes sir!''

''They're leaving in the morning,'' Clint said. ''Make sure you tell them not to leave without me!''

Chapter Four

When there was a knock at his door a couple of hours later, he was sure it would be a newspaperman. Either a new one or one from the lobby who had gotten his nerve up. If it was a newsman, he was going to throw him down the steps so that he hit every one on the way down.

"Get ready, you bastard—" he was saying as he opened the door, but it wasn't a newspaperman.

It was Estralita Martinez, looking much as she had four or five years before, when he'd become involved in a "wet stock" operation on the border.*

"Lita," he said.

"I am not who you expected, yes?" she asked.

"Not who I expected," he agreed, "but welcome, very welcome. Come in."

"Thank you."

She stepped past him into the room, and she even smelled the way he remembered her.

"You haven't changed," he said, and she turned so he could examine her.

She was still small, though more of a woman than a girl now, with the same dark skin and wild black hair. Her eyes, fiery before, now smoldered. She had full lips and perfectly formed, small breasts which could not be contained by the low-cut peasant blouse.

*The Gunsmith #7: The Longhorn War

17

The blouse was off the shoulder, and now she reached up with each hand and hooked an index finger on each side of the blouse to peel it down and away from her breasts.

"It has been a long time," she said. "Much too long."

He agreed. Stepping forward he proceeded to remove his own shirt. He reached out for her and pulled her to him and, as he remembered, her flesh burned him, her nipples scraped his bare chest. He helped her out of her skirt, and she helped him out of his pants, and then they were on the bed and at each other, hands clutching spasmodically, mouths working avidly, hungrily.

"Dios," she breathed, "I want you. . . . Wait . . ." She snaked down until she was able to take his rock hardness into her mouth and, cupping his balls, began to suck, first gently, and then furiously.

"Lita, damn . . ." Clint said, but she did not release him. She reached beneath him to cup his buttocks while she suckled him to the brink of completion, and then she allowed him to slip out of her mouth. She crawled on top of him like a playful monkey and impaled herself on his shaft. As hot as her flesh was, her insides were even hotter, scalding. She covered his face with wet kisses as he reached behind her to cup her buttocks. He controlled their tempo that way, holding her cheeks tight and moving her up and down his rigid cock.

"Dios mío . . ." she breathed, digging her nails into his chest and sitting up. She had the tempo right now, so he slid his hands from beneath her smooth buttocks and palmed her small breasts. She continued to ride him and placed her hands over his, crushing her breasts in the process.

When she began to slam her pelvis against his with bone-jarring force, he knew she was ready. As her body was wracked with waves of pleasure, she began to spout a steady stream of Spanish, none of which Clint understood, but much of which he could guess about.

● ● ●

"How did you find me?" he asked while they lay together, resting. Perspiration was drying on both of them, but that kind of sweat was never unpleasant.

"I heard you were in Lansdale," she said. "Didn't have time to stop over the border and see me?"

"I really didn't," he said. He'd been too busy trying to get Duke back, at the time.*

"You had time to see Laura Kennedy, though, didn't you?" she asked, pinching his thigh painfully.

"That was business," he said. "I needed her to help me with something."

"Like I just helped you with something?" she asked.

Four years ago she'd been able to speak English with just the faintest hint of an accent—when she wanted to . Now her English was almost flawless.

"How is your father?"

"Still alive, if that's what you mean," she said.

"Yes."

"I tracked you here," she said, "that's how I found you."

"That's how they found me too, I suppose," he said.

"Who?"

"The South Americans," he said, and went on to explain the whole thing to her.

"And you are going to go?"

"Yes."

"Because you killed that boy?"

"Yes."

"He forced you."

"The newspapers don't care," he said. "They want to know what number he is."

"Oh."

"Idiots."

"Bastard, you said at the door."

"That too."

*The Gunsmith #28: The Panhandle Search

"I thought you were going to throw me down the steps," she said.

"I would have, if you'd been a newspaperman," he said.

"I guess we are both lucky I was not," she said, snaking her hand beneath the sheets.

"Yes."

"I like what you did to me better than what you would have done to a newspaperman," she said, closing her small fist around him.

"So did I," he agreed.

"When are you leaving?" she asked, snuggling up close to him.

"In the morning," he said. "I left Ramirez a message at the desk."

"You haven't told him yet?"

"No."

"Don't," she said suddenly, propping herself up on her elbow.

"Why?"

"Stay with me," she said, "in Mexico."

"You . . . and your father?" he asked.

"Father is away on business. He won't be back for weeks," she said. "By then you should be able to cross back into Texas without newspapermen hounding you."

"It's a tempting offer," he said, "but no, Lita. Thank you just the same."

She frowned at him, and then her brow smoothed out as she thought she understood. "You want to go after this Devil Cat, don't you? El Gato Diablo. It sounds interesting, almost pretty, in Spanish, doesn't it?"

He frowned now, because maybe she was right. "You've grown up smart, haven't you, Lita?"

"Are you trying to tell me that I wasn't grown up the first time we met?" she asked, squeezing his penis in her hand.

"You've matured," he said, turning to face her, "in more ways than one."

Later she asked, "May I stay the night?" Before he could answer she added, "We may never see each other again. I would like this night to remember."

Moonlight was streaming in through the window, and he was able to make out the expression on her face in the semi-dark room.

"On one condition," he said.

"What?"

"That you at least let me get some sleep."

She pinched the inside of his thigh, then closed her eyes to go to sleep.

Chapter Five

Clint Adams knew very little about South America in general, and Paraguay in particular, and by the time they reached their first stop in that continent, Bogotá, Colombia, what he knew he had learned from the twins, Ernesto and Eduardo. They had insisted on telling him the history of their country, from the Incas to the War of Triple Alliance, which was fought by Paraguay against the larger countries of Brazil and Argentina, as well as Uruguay, and which cost Paraguay almost its entire male population. Clint, however, had interrupted them at one point and told them that he was more interested in Paraguay's present than its past. During the arduous ten-day trip from Bogotá to a small town called Santa Ruiz the twins brought Clint up-to-date on the current situation.

Now there was a war going, to which Paraguay was virtually a spectator and, possibly, an innocent victim. Chile had chosen to attack both Bolivia and Peru, and since Paraguay bordered Bolivia, it occasionally caught some of the spillover violence.

"How close will we get to the fighting during our journey?" Clint asked at one point.

Raphael answered him. "Traveling by land, we should not come in contact with any, but once we reach the Paraguay River we will pass very near both Peru and Bolivia."

"Couldn't we travel overland and avoid the river?" he asked.

Ramirez answered with great care, as if addressing a child

who did not know any better. "That would entail crossing an area which is a vast, hot jungle of lagoons and waterways. This is where the jaguars and crocodiles make their home."

"What about this particular jaguar?"

"We believe he must have come from there, and perhaps finds it easier to make food out of our cattle, rather than fight with the others for the meager supplies of the Chaco."

"Do you have any problems with Indians?"

"There are some Guaraní," Ramirez explained, "but for the most part they keep to themselves. Occasionally we have trouble with bandits, some of whom are deserters from the war, but we are able to handle them."

"But not the cat."

"We have sent many hunters after the Devil Cat, Señor Adams," Ramirez said, "and none have returned."

"That's encouraging."

Santa Ruiz was several days' ride from the Paraguay River. When they reached it, they were expected, with rooms waiting for them.

"Our alliance made the reservations for us," Ramirez explained.

"Alliance?"

"That is what we call it," the man explained. "The ranchers who have been suffering at the, eh, hands of this jaguar have joined to form an alliance. It is by this body that you will be paid."

"I see."

"Please," Ramirez said, "go to your room, rest, bathe. We will meet you later for dinner. In the morning, we will start for the Paraguay river."

"How will we travel the river?" Clint asked.

"There will be a woodburning steamer waiting for us," Ramirez explained. "We will have to dock each night at a settlement to lay in a supply of wood. The trip downriver will take several days."

"I suppose we'd better retire early tonight, then, and get some rest," Clint said.

"Yes."

"Will you have a horse waiting for me?" Clint asked, before going up to his room.

"Oh, yes," Ramirez assured him. "Of course, not one such as yours, but animals will be provided."

"Good. I hope they're better than the ones we rode from Bogotá to here."

That had been Clint's one big sacrifice, as far as he was concerned—leaving Duke behind. If he was going to hunt an animal with a reputation like the Devil Cat, he would have liked to have the big Arabian with him. Besides that, he hated leaving him behind so soon after getting him back from Moose Chandler.*

"I'll see you later," he told Ramirez, and started up to his room.

Checking the number on his key, Clint located his room on the second floor of the ancient hotel. He was about to put the key in the lock when the door opened and a barefoot girl stepped out, walking right into him.

"Hello," he said, as she bounced off. She rebounded back into the room a few steps, where he was able to take a good look at her. She was small, but well built, with pert, proud breasts. Her hair was long and incredibly black, like a moonless night. Her skin was dark and naturally so, her mouth small, but lush. She couldn't have been more than nineteen, and she reminded him a lot of Lita Martinez.

"Hello," he said again.

"I am sorry," she said.

"About what?"

"You will not tell Señor Avilar, please?" she asked, with a worried look in her eyes.

---

*The Gunsmith #28: The Panhandle Search

"Who's he?"

"He owns this hotel."

"Why would I tell him?"

"I am supposed to have your room clean before you get here," she said. "I am not supposed to be in the room when the guest come."

Clint looked around the room from the doorway and said, "Well, it seems to me you did a pretty good job of cleaning the room."

"Thank you, Señor."

"What's your name, little girl?"

She frowned and said, "My name is Ana, and I am not a little girl."

"I'm sorry," Clint said, "I didn't mean any offense . . . and I won't tell Mr. Avilar that you were in my room when I got here."

Her face brightened and she said, "Thank you."

"I'd like to take a bath after I leave my gear in my room," he said, then. "Would you know anything about that?"

She nodded and said, "You come downstairs when you are ready, and I will have hot water waiting."

"All right," he said. "Thank you, Ana."

She gave him a small curtsy, then squeezed past him in the doorway, pressing her pert little breasts against him as she did.

She seemed ingenuous enough, and he doubted that the contact was anything but accidental.

Chapter Six

Clint left his saddlebags and rifle in his room, which was small but comfortable and, thanks to Ana, clean. He removed some clean clothes from his saddlebags and carried them and his gun back down to the first floor.

"Where can I get a bath?" he asked the clerk.

"In the back," the man said, waving a hand. He was concentrating on what appeared to be account books, so he was probably doubling as the bookkeeper. He was young, and Clint doubted that he was the Mr. Avilar that Ana was so concerned about.

"Thank you," Clint said, and the young man waved his hand again in reply.

Clint circled around behind the desk, walked through a curtained doorway and found himself in a long hall. He followed the sounds of water being poured and turned to his right. The second door he came to was open, and Ana was inside, bent over a bathtub, pouring hot water into it. She was facing him, and as she bent over her blouse gaped at her neck, revealing to him her small, rounded breasts, and her brown nipples. As if she sensed his presence she looked up and smiled at him. She made no attempt to straighten up until the pail of water was empty. When she did so, her blouse suddenly molded itself to her damp body, outlining her breasts as if they were bare.

"It is ready," she said.

"Thank you."

He entered the room and draped his gunbelt over the back

of a chair, then pulled it over near the tub, which was surprisingly new. He expected everything in this ancient hotel to be just as old as the building, but obviously that was not the case, especially considering the girl they had cleaning the rooms and drawing guests' baths.

Ana had moved to the other side of the room to set the empty pail down, and was now staring at Clint. He set his clean clothes down on the chair and began to unbutton his shirt.

"Is there anything else I can get you?" the girl asked.

He looked around, saw that there were towels and soap, which was all he really needed, and said, "I don't think so, Ana. Should I let you know when I'm done so you can clean up?"

"Yes, please," she said. She crossed the room to the doorway and, in lieu of a door, pulled a set of curtains closed. For a moment Clint stopped what he was doing and wondered if she was going to stand outside the curtains and watch him the whole time. That thought, however, began to work on his private parts and he abandoned it and continued to undress.

When he was naked he could not help but glance over at the curtains once again. His penis was semi-hard and he thought he saw a movement of the curtains, but it could have been a breeze.

Gingerly, he lifted one foot and submerged it in the tub of hot water, then lifted the other. Gritting his teeth against the heat of the water, he sat down in the tub and allowed the hot water to bake away the aches in his lean frame.

He was seated in the tub so that he could see the door, and his gun was within easy reach. From time to time he thought he caught movement of the curtains again, but was sure it was nothing to be alarmed about. It was either a breeze, or Ana, and if the pretty young girl wanted to peak in at his nakedness, well that was fine with him. He enjoyed watching naked women, so why shouldn't it work both ways? He continued to wash himself, then, feeling no embarrassment. In fact, he was somewhat excited by the prospect of being watched by such a desirable young woman, and his excitement became more and more evident as his semi-hardness quickly became rock hard.

When the water began to get tepid—not to mention black—he stood up, and his erection was as full as it could be without the benefit of a woman's direct involvement. As he stood, he thought he detected the sound of a gasp, or a sharp intake of breath, from outside the curtain, and he was no longer unsure as to whether or not he was being watched.

"What would Mr. Avilar say about this?" he asked aloud. "How does he feel about you watching guests bathe?"

There were a few silent moments, and then the curtains parted and Ana walked in, head bowed.

"I do not usually watch guests bathe," she said with her eyes fixed on the floor.

"Don't worry, Ana," he said, "I don't have any intention of telling Mr. Avilar."

"Thank you," she said.

"Pick up your head, girl," he said. "You've seen all there is to see already. Don't be shy."

For a few moments he thought that she would back out of the room without looking up, but then her eyes began to rise from the floor until she was looking at him, at a certain portion of his anatomy, and in moments she was staring unabashedly.

"Are you a virgin, Ana?" he asked. The entire situation was becoming extremely exciting, especially since there was no door on the room to lock.

She shook her head without removing her eyes from him and said, "I am not . . . but I have never seen such a . . . a . . . I have never seen one like . . . that!"

"You mean as large?"

She nodded and said, "Yes."

"Come closer, then," he invited her.

She took a few small, mincing steps towards him, and then advanced more boldly until she was right in front of him.

"Take a good look, Ana," he said.

She stared at his stiffened, pulsing penis and then tentatively reached out her hand, only to pull it back just short of touching him.

"You can touch it if you like," he heard himself tell her. Fool, he chided himself, anyone could walk in at any moment.

Her touch was like a feather at first as she ran her fingertips around the head, and then along the underside. Becoming even more bold, she hefted his sac in her left hand, while gripping his tool tightly with her right.

"Ah, Ana . . ." he breathed.

"It feels nice?" she asked.

"It feels wonderful," he told her, truthfully, "but if you are making me feel so good, it's only fair that I do the same for you, isn't it?"

"Oh, please," she said, her tone almost beseeching, "make me feel good!"

He reached out to touch her breasts through the fabric of her blouse. He had already noticed that her nipples were distended, forming hard little nubs beneath the blouse. He pulled the neckline of the garment down until her small but perfectly formed breasts bobbed free, and then he flicked at her nipples with his thumbs.

"Oh, *Dios*," she moaned, reminding him even more at that moment of Estralita Martinez. Her eyes were closed and her tongue was between her lips as he continued to fondle her breasts. Her hands on him became frantic, and he was forced to stop her before he splashed all over her.

"Ana," he said, taking hold of her shoulders. He shook her until she opened her eyes and focused on his face. "Get some dry towels," he instructed her.

As if in a daze she walked across the room to a set of shelves and took off two or three towels.

"More," he said, and she removed three more and brought them back to him.

"Spread them on the floor, in two layers," he told her, and she obeyed. The floor was hardwood, and the two layers of towels would soften it just a bit, but it would be enough.

"Come here," he said.

She moved towards him and he pulled her blouse over her head, then removed her skirt.

Now she was as naked as he.

"Lie down on the towels, Ana," he said, "and we'll make each other feel good."

"Yes," she said, and obediently lay down on the towels, on her back.

He knelt beside her and began to fondle her breasts again, and she reached eagerly for his rock hard cock.

She closed her eyes and fondled the length of him in her hands. He leaned over to take one nipple into his mouth, and then sucked so that he could take much of her small breast with it. Her breath caught in her throat.

"Please," she said, tugging at his prick, "please, make me feel good with . . . this!"

"Relax, Ana," he said. She was so delectable that he wanted to take his time with her, but it was too chancy. The room was virtually wide open, and at any minute another guest could come down and discover them, maybe Raphel Ramirez, himself, or maybe her Mr. Avilar, who would probably fire her.

He straddled her small form, gently prodded her moist portal with the swollen head of his erection, and then drove it into her to the hilt.

He didn't know how she did it, but somehow she kept from screaming when it was quite obvious that a scream was welling up from deep inside of her.

He began to take her in long, deep strokes, made deeper still by the hard, unyielding floor beneath the thin bed of towels. She wrapped her legs around his waist and lifted her little butt to eagerly meet his strokes. Their mouths fused together, and with each thrust of his hips, he drove his tongue into her mouth, as if he were having her in two places at once, and she was eagerly sucking him deeper in each place.

When her time came she made a high keening noise deep in her throat, and raked his back with her nails. When he allowed himself to explode inside her, she drummed her heels against his buttocks, and he knew he was going to have bruises to show for it.

She was one energetic little girl, and she milked him dry.

"Dios," she whispered as he withdrew from her.

He rose and helped her to her feet, and then sneaked a glance at the curtained doorway. They had been lucky that no one walked in on them.

"Next time," he said, wiping himself with a damp towel, "we'll do it in my room. Okay?"

"Very okay," she said, with a grin.

As he dressed himself, she picked up all of the towels on the floor and put them aside to be washed. As he was tightening his gunbelt she prepared to empty the tub, and someone walked through the curtained doorway.

"I am sorry," Raphael Ramirez apologized, looking at Clint.

"That's all right," Clint assured him, "I'm finished."

Ramirez looked at the girl and said something in Spanish, to which she nodded. Clint imagined that he was asking for a bath, and she had told him it would be a few minutes while she heated some water. Ramirez was dressed, but as Clint had done, he had brought down some clean clothes with him.

"You'll enjoy your bath, Señor Ramirez," Clint said as he passed the man on the way out. With a fleeting glance at Ana, he added, "I know I enjoyed mine."

Chapter Seven

An hour later Clint met Ramirez and his twin nephews in the hotel lobby. They all looked freshly bathed, but somehow he doubted that they had gotten as much out of their baths as he had out of his.

And then he wondered, *Or had they?*

"Are you ready for dinner, Mr. Adams?" Ramirez asked.

"I am," Clint said, "but I think if I'm going to be spending some more time with you, señor, you should call me Clint."

"We will see," the old man said. Clint hadn't really expected the old man to warm up. There was just enough aristocrat in the Ramirez bloodline, he was sure, to make that impossible.

"Let's go and eat, Clint," Eduardo said, anxiously, "and you can tell us some stories."

The twins had begun calling him by his first name long ago, but he didn't think he wanted to tell them the kind of stories they were looking for.

"You fellas are too old for stories," he said.

"I agree," Ramirez said. "Ernesto, you and your brother go and have dinner together. I will have dinner with Mr. Adams."

"But, Uncle—" Ernesto began to argue.

"You may tell each other stories," the old man said, cutting him off. Both nephews looked longingly at Clint and their uncle, and then Ernesto nodded and said, "Yes, Uncle."

33

"Yes, Uncle," Eduardo echoed, and they walked away.

"Thank you," Clint said.

"They are young," Ramirez said. "Shall we go?"

"You lead the way," Clint said.

He followed Ramirez to a small restaurant which was just as ancient as the hotel. It was run by an elderly couple who were slow bringing the food, but when it came it was worth it.

"We've talked quite a bit about your country, Señor Ramirez," Clint said, "but I'd like to find out something about this cat."

"I can only tell you that he is deadly," Ramirez said, "and that he is the devil incarnate."

Clint had heard that before, specifically about Ole Three Paw, the killer grizzly which one man had even thought of as a god.

"I could use a little more than that, Mr. Ramirez," Clint said. "How many people have seen this animal up close?"

"There is one," Ramirez said, "who has seen the devil cat and lived, but he will be of no use to you."

"Why not?"

"He has been mad ever since that time," Ramirez said.

"Really? Well, I think I'd like to see him, anyway, just on the off chance that he might be able to tell me something."

"As you wish," Ramirez said, stiffly. "I will arrange for you to see him as soon as we reach my ranch."

"Fine," Clint said, "I appreciate that."

"We must do everything we can to assist you, Señor Adams," the old man said. "After all, you are here to save us."

"I'm here to hunt," Clint said. "I hope no one will try and cast me in the role of savior. I have enough problems with my reputation as it is."

"Of course," Ramirez said. "I understand perfectly. Shall we go back to the hotel?"

"I think I'll walk around town a little bit, if you don't

mind," Clint said. "Maybe get a feel for the people of South America. Uh, do they play poker here?"

"I'm sure you will be able to find some games of chance to suit you," Ramirez said. "I will go back to the hotel. I need as much rest as possible before we start our trek to the river tomorrow."

"Of course," Clint said, rising as the older man rose. "I'll be returning to the hotel myself, shortly."

"Good night," Ramirez said.

"Oh, Mr. Ramirez," Clint said then, before the other man could leave. "One more thing."

"Yes?"

"This man who saw the jaguar," Clint said. "Who was he?"

"My son," Ramirez said. "My other son, Mr. Adams. The devil cat has killed one of my sons, and has driven the other mad. Good night."

"Good night," Clint said, sorry that he had asked.

Chapter Eight

Clint hadn't walked two blocks when he found a saloon. Well lit, it was quiet, with no music and only the voices of a few men who were drinking and playing poker. The other men—two at the bar, two at separate tables—simply stayed quiet, drank their drinks and watched the four poker players.

One of the poker players was Eduardo, and one of the men standing at the bar was Ernesto. He was staring at his brother, shaking his head, when Clint approached.

"Ernesto," he said.

"Oh, Señor Clint," he said. "You and my uncle have finished your dinner?"

"Yes," Clint replied. He ordered a beer and turned to face Ernesto. "Your uncle has gone back to the hotel to rest up for tomorrow's trip. That's what we should be doing, as well."

"Uncle is getting older," Ernesto said, watching his brother again. "We are young."

Clint wondered if that "we" were meant to include him.

"I would like to get Eduardo away from that table, though," Ernesto said, then.

"Why?"

"He gambles too much," Ernesto answered, "and he gambles very badly."

"Whose money does he lose?"

"His own."

37

"Then it's pretty much his own decision, isn't it?" Clint asked.

"It should be," Ernesto said, "but Eduardo has not much sense, Clint. I have gotten into the habit of watching out for him."

"Getting him out of trouble?"

"Yes," Ernesto said, "and trouble is what he is heading for right now."

"Why?"

"Because he is winning," Ernesto said.

"Why is that trouble?"

"Because when he wins, he gambles even more badly than when he loses," Ernesto said. "Also, he is playing with a very bad man, who is a very bad loser."

"Which one?"

"The large man with the two bandoliers."

"Who is he?"

"An American who has spent most of his life in South America," Ernesto answered. "He is a mercenary who will work for anyone as long as the money is right."

"Is he any good?"

"He is very good at what he does, but he has a very bad temper," Ernesto explained.

"Does your uncle know about him?"

"Oh, yes. All of the ranchers know Sykes."

"Sykes," Clint repeated, looking at the man in question with interest.

Sykes was a big man, wearing dirty, sweat-stained clothing. His shirt was open, revealing a hard-muscled, massive chest, and his sleeves were rolled up over his bulging biceps. At that moment, he was frowning across the table at Eduardo, who was grinning back over his cards.

"It is your bet, Señor Sykes," they heard Eduardo say.

"I know that, sonny," said Sykes, who appeared to Clint to be in his middle or late thirties. "You've got a lot of my money there in front of you."

"Yes," Eduardo said happily. "I have been very lucky today."

"You sure have," Sykes agreed, "but here's where I get some of it back. I'll bet fifty."

The player to his left folded.

"I will raise fifty," Eduardo said.

The fourth player also folded.

"I was hoping you'd say that," Sykes said. He pushed forward a bundle of paper money and said, "I'll call and raise a hundred."

Eduardo made a show of examining the money Sykes had left in front of him and then said, "If I raise you back, it will most likely break you."

Sykes smirked and said, "I'm ready to take that chance, kid."

"Very well," Eduardo said. "I raise."

Sykes pushed the remainder of his money into the pot and said, "What have you got, kid—not that it matters."

Gleefully, Eduardo laid down his cards and said, "I have four Aces."

"You have four *what?*" Sykes roared. He stared down at Eduardo's cards, and then bellowed, "I have four kings, damn it!"

"That is not good enough, I'm afraid," Eduardo said, happily raking in his winnings.

"That ain't natural," Sykes shouted, standing up. He was at least six foot four, Clint noticed. "Four of a kind twice in one hand ain't natural."

"You were the dealer," Eduardo reminded Sykes, and that only made the big man more angry. On his hip he wore a Colt Walker, and he started to pull it free of its holster.

"I wouldn't," Clint shouted.

Sykes looked over at Clint, his hand resting on the butt of his gun.

"Mind your own business," Sykes advised him.

"I am," Clint said. "That man is a friend of mine, and he won your money fair and square. If you can't lose gracefully, you shouldn't be playing."

"Is that a fact?" Sykes asked. "Well, how about I take you apart first, and then take care of your friend? How does that strike you?"

"I don't think you would be able to do that," Eduardo spoke up, grinning at Sykes.

"And why not?" Sykes demanded.

"Eduardo—" Clint heard Ernesto say warningly beneath his breath, but his brother went on.

"He is famous for his ability to use his gun—" Eduardo began, but Clint was quick to cut him off before he could do further damage.

"That's not important," he said aloud, but when Sykes looked at him this time, it was with suspicion.

"What's your name, friend?" Sykes asked.

"Adams," Clint said, "and I think we'd better resolve this little problem right now."

Clint's seemingly relaxed pose against the bar increased Sykes's suspicions, and slowly the big man moved his hand away from his gun.

"He's got five hundred of my money," Sykes said. "I broke my ass working for that money."

And a few heads, too, Clint bet himself silently. "Then you should have been more careful with how you used it," he said aloud, "and lost it. Make some more, and you can try winning it back."

"I could break you in two with my bare hands, Adams," Sykes said.

"You probably could," Clint agreed, "but you'd have to get close enough, first."

Sykes nodded his head slightly, considering his options. "That's true." His stance became more relaxed, with his hands dangling at his sides. "This isn't the end of this, for any of us. There are three of you, and one of me, so we'll put it off for another time."

"Whenever," Clint said.

"You're an American, Adams," Sykes said. "We should be on the same side, not opposite sides."

"I've only got one side, Sykes," Clint said, "and that's mine."

"Yeah," Sykes said, moving away from the poker table, "that's how I feel, too."

The big man moved towards the door, then turned and said, "Be watching for me, Adams."

"Don't worry," Clint said as the man went out the door, "I will be."

When Sykes was gone Eduardo stood up from the table and told the other two players, "This game is over, until next time."

He put his money inside his hat and walked to the bar, grinning happily.

"That was incredible," he said to Clint. "You talked him out of drawing his gun."

"You almost got someone killed, Eduardo," Ernesto said. "Will you never learn?"

"Sykes would have been the one killed, Nesto," he said to his brother. "Clint would have seen to that."

"Eduardo," Clint said, "put your hat on and keep your mouth shut."

"Wha—"

"As long as I'm here, you will not do any gambling," Clint instructed him. "I am not here to keep you out of trouble, and I think the job may be becoming too big for your brother."

"I can take care of myself," Eduardo said, suddenly sullen.

"You have never been able to before," Ernesto said,

although he looked at his brother with nothing but affection. Eduardo just stared at his brother, remaining sullen and silent. He took the money out of his hat and put his hat on, then stuffed the money into his pockets.

"I think we'd better get back to the hotel and rest for tomorrow's journey," Clint suggested.

"I agree," Ernesto said. "Come, Eduardo. We have more important matters to attend to."

"Perhaps we do," Eduardo agreed. He looked at Clint and said, "I am sorry."

"That's a start, Eduardo," Clint said, touching the younger man's shoulder. "That's a start."

Clint was back in his room, preparing to go to bed when there was a light knocking on his door. He thought it might be Eduardo, looking to apologize further.

He opened the door and found Ana standing out in the hall, still barefoot, still dressed as she had been earlier.

"Hello," he said.

"You are preparing to go to bed?" she asked.

"That's right."

"Good," she said, and walked in. He closed the door and when he turned around she had already discarded her blouse and was dropping her skirt to the floor. The smooth, sleek flesh of her body was nut brown, and her nipples were an even darker brown. They already stood at attention in anticipation.

"You said that next time we would do it in your room," she told him. "Remember?"

"I remember," he said.

She walked to him and removed his already unbuttoned shirt. Dropping it to the floor, she pressed the swollen tips of her breasts against his bare flesh, burning him, closing her eyes against the sensation that this simple act caused.

"I am ready," she said.

"Yes," he said, sliding one hand between her legs, "you certainly are."

"What time must you leave?" Ana asked him, many hours later.

It was not yet daylight, but one look at the window told Clint that the sun was not long from rising. It hadn't actually been set, their time of departure, but he assumed that Ramirez would want to get as early a start as possible.

"Probably first light," he replied.

She tangled her fingers in his pubic hair and said, "That is not so long from now."

"No, it's not," he said.

"Could we . . . ?" she asked, sliding her hand even lower.

"Again?" he asked.

"Yes," she said, "please."

He rolled over and began to kiss her breasts, running his tongue along the valley between them, collecting the salt of her perspiration. As he sucked on her nipples, she moaned and cradled his head in her hands.

He slid his hand down until it was nestled between her legs, fingers busy.

"I am ready," she told him, "oh, I am ready. . . ."

"Seems to me you're always ready," he replied, straddling her.

"Only with you," she said, wrapping her arms and legs around him. She gasped as he entered her and then said, "Only with you," again.

He took her easily this time, slowly, drawing it out and making it last. Their last coupling had been violent, and he had scratches and welts on his back to prove it. This time, he was going to go slow, and make it last.

She clutched at him as he slowly stroked in and out of her,

and eventually she asked him to go faster, as he knew she would.

"No," he said.

"Why?"

"We've gone fast," he said. "Now I want to go slow."

"I can't . . ." she gasped. "I can't take it. It feels too good."

"It can never feel too good," he told her. "Just relax and let me do it."

He slid his hands beneath her buttocks, cupping them, and continued to take her in slow, long strokes. He felt himself swelling even more inside of her, until he felt he might become too big for her. That was when he increased the tempo. . . .

"Oh, yes," she moaned, "that's wonderful . . ."

She clung to him and was working at his back with her nails again.

"You're going to tear me to pieces, girl," he said.

"I can't help it," she said, "I can't . . . ohhhh . . ."

She was coming then, going wild beneath him, and he surrendered himself and began to spurt into her, an incredible torrent of semen that was almost painfully milked from him.

"Oh, Clint," she said, "take me with you."

The sun was coming up and he could see her face clearly, now.

"I can't," he said, disengaging himself from her and sitting up. "I can't, Ana, not where I'm going."

She lowered her eyes and said, "I am sorry I asked. I did not mean . . . I only wanted to leave here, and I thought . . ."

He touched her arm and she looked at him.

"You're better off here than where I'm going," he assured her, and she nodded her head.

"Will you come back this way?"

"When I've finished, yes, I suppose so," he said.

"I will wait, then," she said. "We will say good-bye when you come back."

"That will give me something to look forward to," he said, cupping her chin in his hand. He leaned over and kissed her gently, and said, "Thank you."

Chapter Nine

Ana had drifted off to sleep by the time Clint was ready to leave, so he slipped out of bed without waking her, dressed, and left the room with his gear. Ramirez and the twins were waiting for him in the lobby.

"Good morning," he greeted them.

"I have arranged for horses," Ramirez told him. "They are being held at the livery stable."

"I'll just settle up my bill and be along," Clint said, turning towards the desk.

Ramirez said something to the twins in Spanish, and they nodded and left. Ramirez moved in next to Clint at the desk.

"Ernesto told me what you did for Eduardo last night," the old man said without looking at Clint.

"He did?" Clint said. He assumed that the old aristocrat was working himself up to say thank you, so he kept quiet and just waited.

"I . . . appreciate what you did," Ramirez said. "You saved his life."

"Maybe," Clint said, handing the clerk some money.

"Eduardo does not carry a gun," Ramirez said, "and if he did, he would not know what to do with it."

"He should," Clint said, picking his gear up and turning to face Ramirez. "A young man should know how to handle a gun in order to protect himself."

47

"If you carry a gun, eventually you will kill someone with it," Ramirez said.

"There's always that possibility," Clint said. "On the other hand, if Eduardo had had a gun last night, he might not have found himself in any danger."

"If he had been wearing a gun, it might have provoked the man into shooting instantly, without warning."

"All right," Clint said, "so we agree that a gun could deter or instigate a confrontation. Should we go now, Mr. Ramirez?"

"Yes," Ramirez said. The old man looked unconvinced, and Clint knew that no amount of talking on his part would change his mind. He'd argued with people like Ramirez before, people who saw no good in guns at all. Even the Gunsmith, who had seen more damage done with guns than anyone else, knew that they had their good uses, too.

They walked to the livery, where they found Ernesto and Eduardo waiting with four saddled horses.

"They look like buzzard bait," Clint said, casting a critical eye on the skinny, stringy horses.

"It was the best they had," Ernesto said.

"I hope you can do better for me once we reach your ranch, Mr. Ramirez," Clint said, facing the old man.

"Have no fear," Ramirez said. "I have excellent horses on my ranch. I would not send you after El Gato Diablo on anything less."

"I hope not," Clint said. He picked out the best of the poor lot, slid his rifle into the scabbard of the worn saddle, and climbed up on the horse's back. He swore he could almost hear the creature grunt beneath his weight.

"Shall we get started, gentlemen?" he suggested. "I don't know how long this . . . horse . . . can put up with my weight, let alone his own."

As the others mounted up, Ramirez said, "It won't have to put up with it for very long, Señor."

"What do you mean?"

"When we reach a certain point we will reach a sort of dry swampland. The brush and undergrowth will be too thick for the horses."

"You mean we'll have to travel on foot?"

Ramirez nodded.

"Until we reach the river," he said. "The boat will be waiting there."

How dry could anything called a "swamp" be? Clint wondered. He remembered walking through a swamp in New Orleans,* and the nag beneath him started to look better with every passing moment.

As Clint, Ramirez and the twins rode out of town they were watched from a hotel window by Brad Sykes.

"What's so interesting out the window, honey?" the whore in his bed asked.

"Nothing that concerns you," he replied without looking at her.

"Then come on back to bed, Brad, honey," the girl said. "We ain't finished already, are we?"

Sykes turned and looked at the big, dark-haired girl on his bed. She was the only whore he could find in town who was able to keep up with him. She was the only one big enough for him. He looked admiringly at her big breasts and thighs, and could feel his massive penis beginning to twitch, but he said, "I'm sorry, honey, but yeah, we are finished . . . for now."

He walked across the room, picked up his pants and began to put them on.

"What's more important than these?" she asked, cupping her breasts in her hands and holding them out to him, like a sacred offering.

"Money, sweetheart," he said. He was tempted by her,

*The Gunsmith #10: New Orleans Fire

there was no doubt about that, but money was the overriding concern in life for Brad Sykes.

"There aren't many things in life more important than these, Beverly," he said, reaching out his big hands to tweak her nipples, "but money is one of them."

He finished dressing, strapped on his gun, and hurriedly left his room. He didn't want the four men to get too big a head start on him.

He didn't want his five hundred dollars to get too far away from him.

When Ana awoke and found Clint gone she dressed quickly and ran from the room. She thought that maybe she could catch him at the stable and make one last plea to go with him.

When she got to the livery it was empty. Not even the liveryman was around. She looked through the stalls and found four of them empty. She sank to her knees on the hay in one stall, out of sight, and hung her head. At the sound of voices, her head snapped up and she listened intently, because she had heard the name "Adams."

"What do we do when we find them, Sykes?" a man asked. Ana knew the name Sykes, and she'd heard about what happened at the saloon the night before. She continued to listen and dared not breathe for fear that someone might hear her.

"They got my money, Josh," Sykes's voice said. "I want it back, and I don't really care how."

"I'll get the rest of the boys, then," Josh said. "Should we meet you back here?"

"Yeah—no, let me come with you. If we split up we'll find them faster."

"You think six of us are enough?" the man called Josh asked.

''Plenty,'' Sykes said. ''The only one who'll give us any trouble is Adams, and how many men does it take to kill one . . .''

The voices trailed off after that, but Ana had heard enough to know that Clint was in grave danger. Sykes was a dangerous man, and he meant to kill Clint. She couldn't just stand by and let that happen. She had to do something.

She left her hiding place in the empty stall and hurried to one of the other horses. She was a good rider and had no need of a saddle. She turned the horse around, grabbed a fistful of mane and swung atop gracefully. She didn't know exactly how much of a head start Clint had on her, but she had to reach him and warn him, and when she did, she'd stay with him.

Chapter Ten

"I did not realize that horses needed so much rest," Ernesto said.

They were stopped for what seemed like the hundredth time to give their ancient mounts a rest.

"They do when they're this old," Clint said.

"How old are they?"

"Mine's twelve if he's a day," Clint said, "and he's the baby of the bunch." He looked up at the sky, which told him it was past midday, and said, "We'd have been better off on foot from the beginning."

Ramirez and Eduardo came walking over to where Clint and Ernesto were sitting and the old man said, "I think we had better get started again."

"Are we expecting to reach the river before nightfall?" Clint asked, standing up.

"We had expected to, yes," Ramirez said.

"Now we hope to," Eduardo said, and the old man threw him a dirty look.

Ernesto stood up and said, "We had better get to the swamp before nightfall, in any case."

"Then let's get started," Clint said. He picked up the reins from his horse, who seemed to eye him dubiously, and hauled himself into the saddle once again.

As they continued on, Ramirez and Eduardo took the point and Clint and Ernesto followed.

"What do you know about this cat, Ernesto?" Clint asked.

Ernesto seemed to shudder at the mention of the Devil Cat and he said, "I have never seen him, Clint, but I have seen his work."

"When?"

"I saw what he did to my cousin. Aldo was ripped into pieces, and the sight drove his brother, Alonzo, mad."

"How about the old man?" Clint asked.

"Uncle?"

"How is he standing up to all this?"

"My uncle has always been a very strong man. . . ." Ernesto said, and Clint had the feeling that there was an unspoken "but" at the end of it.

"But?" he asked, supplying it.

Ernesto looked at him, then ahead at his uncle. In a low voice which Clint had to strain to hear he said, "I think that my uncle might be at the end of his rope, if I am using the correct phrase?"

"You are if you mean that he's about ready to crack," Clint said.

"To crack?" Ernesto said, mulling the term over. "Yes, I think that sounds right. He has put up an incredible fight, and he insisted to the members of the alliance that he be allowed to make the trip to the United States. They felt that he was too old to make the trip, but they could not sway him. They finally convinced him to take along my brother and myself."

"I'm sure that was a great help," Clint said, remembering that Eduardo had a knack for getting into trouble.

"Uncle likes to feel that he needs no one," Ernesto said.

"Maybe he's just trying to convince himself of that," Clint said.

"I believe you are right," Ernesto said, still speaking in low tones.

At that point Ramirez tuned in his saddle to look at the two of them, and Ernesto sat straight up with a very guilty look on his face. Ramirez frowned, but said nothing and faced front again.

"He does not like to be talked about behind his back," Ernesto said to Clint.

"No one does," Clint said. "Let's talk about the cat."

Again the mention of the cat seemed to cause a shudder to run through the young man's body.

"He is a monster, a demon," Ernesto said.

"Yes," Clint said, "but do you think we could get a little more precise about him? Is he much larger than a normal jaguar? How large does a normal jaguar grow?"

"They vary in size," he said. "Some grow as large as a North American mountain lion, some even larger. Have you ever seen a Bengal tiger?"

"Once," Clint replied, recalling the one time he had been to a circus back East, a long time ago. "They're huge. Do you mean to say that jaguars have been known to grow that large?"

"This one seems even larger," Ernesto said.

"Uh-huh," Clint said, nodding. "He's become sort of a legend, right?"

"Oh, yes."

And we all know how big legends can grow, he added to himself. *Sometimes even as big as a Bengal tiger.*

Chapter Eleven

The first shot struck Clint's horse in the knee of the right foreleg, shattering it. As the horse staggered Clint moved swiftly, so that he was off the animal as it fell.

"Wha—" Ramirez cried out. His horse had stopped at the sound of the shot, and then reared up on his hind legs, expending more energy than he had in years. Ramirez fell from the saddle, striking the ground with an audible thud.

Clint hit the ground rolling, to present as difficult a target as possible, at the same time shouting, "Down, everybody get down!"

"Uncle—" Ernesto shouted. He was dismounting as the second shot sounded, and the bullet struck him in the back, high up on the right side. He fell against his horse, who moved away from him, allowing him to fall to the ground.

"Nesto!" Eduardo shouted. He was still astride his horse, and was unsure which of the fallen men he should rush to aid.

"Eduardo, get off that horse!" Clint shouted.

"Where—"

"Help your uncle," Clint called. "I'll get your brother."

Having been told what he should do Eduardo sprang into action. He jumped from his mount and rushed to his uncle while hot chunks of lead punched into the ground around him.

Clint had pulled his gun, but holstered it now as he hurried to Ernesto's side.

"Ernesto!"

"Clint," Ernesto moaned, "it hurts."

"Be thankful for that," Clint said as he grabbed the boy beneath his arms and dragged him to the nearest cover, a clump of bushes in a small gully.

"Clint—"

"Relax," Clint said, turning him on his left side, "let me take a look."

"My uncle," Ernesto said through clenched teeth, "I saw him fall."

"Eduardo is looking after your uncle," Clint said.

"Eduardo, he is all right?"

"They're both fine," Clint said, hoping he was right. "Now keep quiet, I can't hear the bullets."

There were plenty of them to hear. Whoever was firing at them had help. From the sound of it, Clint guessed four, maybe five different guns.

He ripped Ernesto's shirt away from his wound and inspected it. The bullet had gone through cleanly and damage was minimal. All he had to do at the moment was stop the bleeding. He tore Ernesto's shirt into strips and used it to pack and secure the wound.

"Don't move around, Ernesto," Clint said. "I've stopped the bleeding for now."

He helped the wounded man into a more comfortable, seated position and said, "Keep your head down."

"The others—"

"I'll check on them," Clint promised. He pulled his gun out of his holster and peered out from cover. The firing had stopped, at least temporarily. The shooters were probably waiting for something to shoot at.

"Eduardo!" Clint called.

"Yes," the other twin's voice replied. Apparently, he had

found cover at least as good as Clint's for himself and his uncle.

"Are you or your uncle hit?"

"No," Eduardo replied. "We are not shot."

"Okay, just sit tight."

Clint crouched down and told Ernesto, "I'm going to have to leave you."

"Where are you going?"

"I've got to find out if whoever was shooting at us is still out there," Clint said, "and if they are, where they are."

"They are going to kill us," Ernesto said.

"Maybe they're going to try," Clint said, "but it isn't going to be easy. Do you have a gun?"

"No."

"Does your brother, or your uncle have one?" Clint asked, already knowing the answer.

"No," Ernesto said. "Uncle has a rifle, but that is only in the event we run into the Devil Cat."

"I see," Clint said. He doubted that Ramirez would have had the time, or the presence of mind, to have grabbed that rifle on his way down to the ground.

Clint reached inside his shirt and took out the Colt New Line he carried as a belly gun. It had become second nature for him to tuck the little gun inside his belt each day.

"Can you handle this without shooting yourself in the foot?" he asked Ernesto.

"I can shoot a gun," Ernesto replied indignantly.

"Fine," Clint said, handing him the little Colt. "Does your uncle know about that?"

"My uncle does not have to know everything," Ernesto answered.

"Sure," Clint said. "All right, now keep your head down and don't use that gun unless you really need it."

"What's going to happen?"

"We'll just have to wait and see, Ernesto," Clint said. "Try not to move around a lot or you'll start bleeding again."

"Am I going to die?" Ernesto asked. "I have never been shot before."

"None of us is going to die, if I can help it," Clint said.

He got to his knees and peered about, trying to locate whoever had been shooting at them. He couldn't see a thing, and knew he was going to have to expose himself in order to find them.

"Here goes," he said, only half aloud. He picked out a small formation of rocks and took off at a dead run for it.

The first shot did not help him any, except to make him run a little faster, but when the second shot came, he was able to pinpoint its source.

He dove headfirst for the rock formation as a slug hit one of them, spraying him with stone chips.

"I got one of you," he said to himself. There was a large stand of solid-looking brush about twenty yards away from which he had seen the barrel of a rifle protruding. There was at least one man there.

"Now all I have to do," he went on, "is find the rest of you before you realize that you're only facing one gun."

When they realized that, he had no doubt that they'd rush him, and then it would be all over—and he'd never even know why.

At the sound of the shots Ana, who till then had been hopelessly lost, caught her breath. As the shots continued she halted her horse and listened, trying to locate the direction the sound was coming from. When she thought she had it she turned the horse and urged him forward, using her knees and heels.

"Come on, *caballo*," she urged, "we could not get there

in time to warn him, perhaps we can get there in time to help him.''

Barefoot and unarmed, she rushed to help the Gunsmith face an unknown number of hidden gunmen.

Ramirez, bleeding from the back of his head, made a move as if to rise, and Eduardo put his hands on his uncle's shoulders and pushed him down.

"We must do something," Ramirez insisted.

"You are in no condition, Uncle," Eduardo told him, "and we are unarmed."

Eduardo got to his knees so he could look at the rock formation Clint was now crouched behind.

"It is up to him to get us all out alive," he said, "and from everything we have heard and read, I believe he can do it."

Chapter Twelve

Here he was, Clint thought, in South America to hunt some kind of Devil Cat, but faced now with a familiar, old danger instead of a new one. Well, he certainly hadn't traveled all this way to die at the hands of an unknown gunman for an unknown reason.

But maybe that reason wasn't so hard to figure out. How many people had he gotten mad at him since he got here? Only one: Sykes.

"Sykes," he called out. "Are you out there, Sykes?"

His three comrades all jumped at the sound of his voice, and both Eduardo and Ernesto recognized the name he was calling out.

"What is it?" Ramirez said. "Who is he calling to?"

"Sykes," Eduardo said, "the man from the saloon."

"Is that what this is about?" Ramirez demanded. "A man angry because he lost money in a poker game? We are to die for that, after all we have been through?"

"We are not going to die, Uncle," Eduardo said. He reached inside of his shirt, where he carried his money. "I will give him back his money, and he will let us go."

As Eduardo started to stand up his uncle placed a restraining hand on his arm.

"We are not yet sure that it is this man who is shooting at us," he warned. "Let us wait and see."

They waited together, listening intently.

"Sykes!" Clint called out again. "I knew you were a sore loser, Sykes, but this is ridiculous!"

"He knows it's you," Josh said to Sykes. "How?"

"He doesn't know," Sykes said, holding his gun ready should Adams stick his head up long enough. "He's just guessing."

"What are we gonna do?" Josh asked. "How long are we gonna wait?"

"We don't know what kind of shape they're in," Sykes said, "or how well armed. Why don't you rush them and find out?"

"Ha! Not me, pal! I ain't in no hurry to die, not for your five hundred dollars."

Sykes threw Josh a look that made the other man almost wince.

"There's more to this than just the money," Sykes said.

Sykes and Josh were not in the stand of brush that Clint had spotted earlier, but they were not far removed from it. They were secreted in a depression of their own, like the one where Clint had dragged Ernesto.

"Let's open fire on Adams's position," Sykes said. "The others will follow. Maybe we'll get lucky and hit him, or at least drive him out into the open."

"Whatever you say, Sykes," Josh said.

"Open fire!"

Clint was about to call out again when several guns opened fire on him. He ducked down as far as he could while bullets bounced off the rocks he'd taken cover behind. Once or twice he was showered with stone chips, some of which stung his neck and hands, but no serious damage was done. They were trying to panic him, force him out into the open, but he wasn't reacting. He was calmly waiting for an opening of his own, one which would get them all out of this mess.

If he was patient enough, the opening would come.
It would have to.

"Uncle," Eduardo said.

"Yes?" the old man replied, wearily.

"Your rifle," his nephew said. "On your horse."

"What about it?"

"I can see your horse," Eduardo said, and indeed he
could. The horse had not wandered far off after the initial
shots had been fired. Perhaps he was just too old and tired to
run any farther, even frightened as he must have been.

"If I can reach it—"

"You'd be killed before you could take two steps,"
Ramirez said.

"I must try, Uncle."

"Why?" Ramirez asked. "You said yourself it is up to
Adams. This is what he does best, is it not? Gunfights?"

"Still, Uncle," Eduardo said, "I must try."

"Nephew, why must you always be so foolhardy?"
Ramirez said, shaking his head until he realized that the
movement caused him pain.

Eduardo looked at his uncle and thought that perhaps he
was right. He *was* foolhardy, but he hoped that in this case it
would work to their advantage.

"I am going to try, Uncle," he said. "You keep low, as
Clint suggested."

"Go ahead, then," the old man said, "get killed. My sons
are dead, Nesto is probably dead, we will all be dead soon."

"Uncle," Eduardo said, before the old man could continue.

"Yes?"

Eduardo responded with a term he had learned during their
trip to the United States: "Shut up."

Chapter Thirteen

Clint looked out during a momentary lapse in the shooting but ducked his head down again as the lead commenced flying once again. He looked behind him once and thought he spotted Ernesto's head peering up from hiding, before he realized that that was not where he'd left the wounded twin. It was Eduardo whose head he saw, and he waved at the second twin to get down.

"Crazy fool," he said to himself, when instead of getting down, Eduardo eased even further into view.

"Get down!" Clint shouted, but Eduardo shook his head and pointed. Clint looked where he was pointing and saw what Eduardo meant to do. He was going to make a try for Ramirez's rifle.

Clint shook his head at Eduardo, but knew from the look on the youth's face that it would do no good.

Have the good sense to wait until I give you cover, Clint said inside his head. He eased up and when the first shot was fired at him he proceeded to pull the trigger of his modified colt as fast as it would go, firing off five rapid-fire shots. He was vaguely aware of Eduardo running behind him, but couldn't take the chance of sneaking a look. After he'd fired his fifth shot he ducked back down again with his back against the rock and saw that Eduardo had made it. He was fighting the horse to make it stand still, then pulled the rifle free as their attackers began to fire again.

Clint had been reloading the whole time, and now he turned around to fire again, giving Eduardo cover to make it back to his uncle. Instead, the twin ran as hard as he could in a zigzag fashion until he reached Clint's cover, which was barely wide enough to accommodate both of them.

"You should have gone back where you were," Clint said.

"I want to help," Eduardo replied.

"Can you shoot that thing?"

"Yes," Eduardo said, and as if to prove a point he clumsily snapped off a wild shot in the direction of their assailants.

"Okay, hold it," Clint said. "Don't waste the ammo."

"What shall I shoot at?"

"Nothing, yet," Clint said. Now that they had two guns instead of one, he decided not to be so patient anymore.

In the center of the clearing they had been in just before they were fired on lay his mount. The horse's knee had been shattered, but as it had fallen three or four other slugs had struck it, putting it out of its misery. Now it was only good for one thing.

Cover.

"All right," Clint said, "this area is not big enough for the both of us."

Eduardo had read enough American dime novels to know what that meant.

"You want me to leave?" he asked in horror.

"No," Clint said, "you're staying, I'm leaving."

"Where are you going?"

"I'm going to try and get closer," Clint said. "First I'm going to get up and run over there to the dead horse and get my rifle, and you're going to cover me."

"With what?"

Clint looked at him for a second until he determined that the question was a serious one.

"You're going to shoot your rifle in that direction," Clint said, "at that large stand of brush, while I run to the horse."

"I understand."

"Fire four or five shots," Clint said. "I don't want you using all of your bullets. Understand?"

"Yes."

Clint ejected the empty shells from his Colt and reloaded swiftly, and he saw that this relatively simple procedure had captured Eduardo's attention, and impressed him.

"Eduardo," he said, "keep your eyes out there. Any moment those men might rush us, and we have to be ready."

Eduardo swallowed hard and nodded. "My brother," he said, then, "how is Nesto?"

"He's fine," Clint told him. "How is your uncle?"

"He is all right," Eduardo answered. "He struck his head when he fell, and he is acting . . . strangely . . . but I believe he is all right."

Clint let the part about Ramirez acting strangely pass, for the moment. It seemed the optimistic thing to do.

"All right," Clint said, getting up on his haunches, "when I say 'now,' you fire four or five shots out there, and no more. Understand?"

"I understand," Eduardo said, getting to his knees and holding his rifle ready.

"Now!" Clint said, and sprinted for the fallen horse while Eduardo gave him cover. He was aware of lead flying around him like so many buzzing bees, but since none of them stung him, he tried not to concern himself. He slid the last few feet until he was lying behind the carcass.

Luck was with him in that when the horse fell he did not fall with the rifle underneath. Clint holstered his revolver and pulled the Springfield free. He looked over at Eduardo, who had stopped firing and ducked his head. He looked back at the place where he'd left Ernesto, who was holding a gun that was useless at any sort of distance. Then he looked over at where Ramirez was, unarmed and "acting strangely."

He devoted a split second to thinking of the last time he had been in a spot as hopeless, then gave it up.

"Sykes," he called, "somebody's got to make a move, Sykes, or we'll be here forever. Let's get it over with!"

He jacked a shell into the chamber and, peering over the ribs of the dead horse, waited for a response.

"Sykes, he's got a point," Josh said. "We got to make some kind of a move, don't we?"

"Why?" the big man asked. "Why do we have to make the move? We're holding all the cards, Josh."

"Cards," Josh said, wiping the sweat from his brow. "That's what got us out here in this heat in the first place."

"Just sit tight, Josh," Sykes said. "They can't last. One of them was hit."

"Are you sure?"

"I hit him," Sykes said. "I'm the only one who hit a goddamn thing, so yes, I'm sure."

"What about the others?"

Sykes looked at Josh, then said, "Okay, maybe you're right—just this once."

"Thanks."

"You go over and tell Squint and Dooley to circle around and get behind them. Tell them to start firing when they get there, just to let us know."

"Right," Josh said.

"Well, go ahead."

"Uh, are you gonna cover me?" Josh asked, nervously. "I'll be in the open for a few seconds."

"I'll cover you," Sykes assured him, "not that you really need it. The only man who can use a gun is pinned down out there behind a dead horse."

"Yeah, but—"

"Go ahead, Josh," Sykes said, "now."

As Josh ran into the open, heading for the large stand of brush, Sykes fired one or two half hearted shots in the direction of the dead horse. In spite of this, the Gunsmith trained his rifle on the moving man, and nailed him with a single shot.

Clint saw the man jerk into the air, as if pulled up by some invisible string, and then fall to the ground. As he did, he felt something tug at his shoulder, and dropped back down behind the dead horse.

His shoulder was bleeding from a nick, barely as serious as a bee sting, so this exchange had been a fair one.

How many of them would go this way, though? he wondered.

As he was trying to decide what to do next, he became aware of the sound of hoofbeats, and then someone rode into the clearing on the dead run.

It was Ana.

The girl was riding into something she had no conception of, and unless he did something she was riding to her death.

In that next split second, Clint decided that he had to go for all or nothing.

"Clint!" Ana shouted, when she spotted him. She turned her horse toward him, and he immediately stood up, making an easy target of himself. By doing so, he gave her a chance to keep alive.

As the Gunsmith stood up, Sykes couldn't believe his luck. The girl had been a distraction riding in that way, but now she was going to be the death of Clint Adams. Sykes was certain that when that man was dead, the others would be as good as dead.

Sykes extended his powerful arm, sighted down the barrel of his Walker Colt, cocked the hammer and pulled the trigger.

Chapter Fourteen

As Clint moved to his left, away from the dead horse and towards Ana, he felt Sykes's bullet whip by his ear. Had he been a split second slower, he would have been dead.

He continued to move towards Ana and the approaching horse, waiting for her to get close enough to grab. As he stepped in front of the horse, Ana pulled on the animal's mane to slow its progress.

"Down!" Clint shouted to her, grabbing the horse's head.

"What's happen—" she started to shout, but he gave her no chance to go further.

"Down," he said, taking her by the arm and pulling her off the horse's back. "Over there!" he shouted. He pushed her towards the dead horse, hoping she was smart enough to know what he wanted her to do.

Without pausing to look back at her he grabbed a fistful of mane and swung himself astride the tired animal. Clint only hoped that the bag of bones underneath him had enough energy left for what he was planning.

Using the pressure of his knees, Clint urged the horse in the direction the shots were being fired from, with his rifle in his left hand, and his revolver in his right. As the horse labored toward the stand of brush, Clint began firing with each hand, using a flick of the wrist to jack a new round into the rifle chamber. He knew it was a crazy move, but he didn't see any other alternatives.

• • •

"Jesus," one of the men hidden in the stand of brush said, "he's crazy!"

"He's heading right for us," the other man said. "Get him!"

"I'm trying," the other man said, but the sight of the man riding straight for them, as if their guns didn't exist, so unnerved both men that their shots were going wild.

"I'm getting out of here!" the first man finally said, when his revolver was empty.

"What about Sykes?"

"What about him?" the first man called, and the second man shrugged, and followed.

There were two other men hidden behind rocks who, noticing that the first two men were fleeing, wondered if perhaps it wasn't the right thing to do. The man on the horse didn't seem worried about their bullets at all, and that just wasn't natural.

It wasn't human!

Sykes fired two shots at Clint and the horse, and one bullet struck the horse in the chest. As the horse stumbled, Clint jumped clear, holding on to both of his guns. It wasn't healthy to be Clint Adams's horse, that day.

Seeing that Clint was down, Sykes stepped clear of his cover to take what he thought would be an easy shot. At that moment, Eduardo stood up and fired the remaining bullets in his rifle. The slugs missed Sykes, but as they whipped by the big man he suddenly realized that Josh was dead, and the other men had abandoned him. He looked over at Eduardo and had no way of knowing that the rifle he was holding was now empty.

"Damn you!" he shouted, and he was not only shouting at Clint, but at his own cowardly men, as well. "Damn all of you. I'm not done yet!"

He threw one last shot at Clint Adams and then turned and ran towards his horse before the other man could regain his balance.

Next time, he seethed, next time he'd have some real men with him, and things would be different.

Chapter Fifteen

"That was incredible," Eduardo shouted, running up behind Clint.

Clint turned to look at Eduardo, then got to his feet, holstering his gun. He paused briefly to look at the dead horse, then went to meet Eduardo.

"Get back to cover," he said, "just in case somebody's still around."

"But you frightened them away!" Eduardo said. "That was marvelous!"

"It was crazy," Clint said, "and it was lucky. Let's see about your brother and your uncle."

"And the girl," Eduardo said, pointing. Ana was standing up and moving away from the dead animal she had been hiding behind. "She is lovely," he added.

"Yes, she is," Clint said. "Why don't you take her over by your uncle, and I'll see to your brother."

"All right."

Eduardo walked over to Ana while Clint hurried back to where he'd left Ernesto.

"Ernesto—" he called. As he moved into the gulley Ernesto suddenly seemed to come awake, and he pointed the Colt New Line at the Gunsmith.

"Easy!" Clint shouted, holding one hand out in front of him. "Take it easy, Ernesto. It's all right."

The boy's eyes seemed to clear suddenly, and he frowned at the Gunsmith. "Clint?"

"Yeah, it's me," Clint said. He stepped forward quickly and snatched the New Line from Ernesto's hand. "It's me, and everything is okay."

"I'm sleepy," Ernesto said.

"I know," Clint said, "I know. Just take it easy."

Ernesto closed his eyes and Clint studied him. He didn't like his color, and thought that he was probably in shock. They had to get him some medical attention as soon as possible.

He left Ernesto and went over to see how the others were.

"Are you all right, Clint?" Ana asked anxiously as he approached.

"I'm fine, Ana," he said. "Give me a few minutes and we'll discuss what you're doing here."

He stepped past her to where Eduardo was helping Ramirez to his feet.

"Are you all right?" he asked the old man.

"Fine," Ramirez answered, "I am fine. Stop fussing," he said to Eduardo.

"He has a bump on his head, and appears to be dizzy," Eduardo said.

The old man did seem to be unsteady on his feet.

"That's great," Clint said. Ernesto was in no shape to walk and Ramirez was shaky. How the hell were they going to make it to the river, and beyond?

"Eduardo," Clint said, "see if you can round up the horses—the ones that are still alive."

"Yes," Eduardo said, "but my uncle—"

Ramirez was leaning on his nephew, in spite of insisting that he was all right.

"Ana," Clint called.

"Yes?" she asked, moving to his side.

"Would you help Señor Ramirez, please?"

"Of course," she said, moving to the old man's side. If she could be of use, she thought, Clint would let her stay with him. She took the old man's arm from Eduardo, who then went in search of the three remaining horses.

"Stay here," Clint told Ana and Ramirez. "I'll be right back."

He turned and began walking across the clearing. He wanted to take a look at the man he had killed.

The dead man was lying on his stomach, with his legs drawn up beneath him. Apparently, he had not died immediately, or easily. Clint turned him over and began to go through his pockets but came up with no more than a two-bit piece with a hole in the center. Most likely a lucky piece, only the luck seemed to have run out the hole. He pocketed it and stood up. The man's gun, an old Navy Colt, had fallen a few feet from him, and Clint tucked it into his belt. The dead man didn't have anything to help their situation, except . . .

"I've got the horses," Eduardo said, coming up behind him, "but there are only three."

"Wrong," Clint said. "There are four."

"Where did the other one come from?" Eduardo asked, looking puzzled.

"From him," Clint said, pointing to the dead man. "It's got to be around here somewhere, so let's find it."

If it was around, he thought, it would be better than any of the three nags they had now, but considering that they had two injured people, and one person more than they started with, how much would that help?

Chapter Sixteen

They found the man's horse not far away. It hadn't run off because it was tied up, and none of the fleeing men had thought to release it.

"Let's take him over with the rest," Clint told Eduardo.

"What are we going to do now?"

"We have to get to the river, where your uncle has the boat waiting," Clint said. "Your brother needs medical attention, and your uncle may too, but if we go back, we might run into those men again, and not be so lucky."

"Lucky?" Eduardo asked. "It was not luck, Clint. It was your skill and courage—"

"Luck," Clint said, interrupting him. "We have to keep going and get to your uncle's ranch as soon as possible."

"There are five of us, and four horses," Eduardo said. "What will we do?"

"What I'd like to do is send the girl back," Clint said.

"On foot?" Eduardo asked in horror. "You could not do that, Clint."

"No," Clint agreed, "I couldn't. We'll have to take her with us. That means that somebody has to walk."

"I will walk," Eduardo said, pounding on his chest with his fist.

"We could ride double if we had better horses," Clint said, "but those nags would never last."

"This is a good animal, is it not?" Eduardo asked, indicating the dead man's horse.

Clint looked at it. Compared to Duke, it was a nag, but at least it was better than what they had. Also, with the dead man's rifle and handgun, they were better armed than they had been before.

"It's all right," Clint said. "We'll put your brother on this one."

"How is he?" Eduardo asked with a worried look on his face.

"He's lost a lot of blood and he may be in shock," Clint said. "He's lucky that the wound itself is not more serious."

"It should be me," Eduardo said.

"That's very gallant, but it doesn't do any good," Clint said.

"No," Eduardo said, "you don't understand. That was Sykes who was shooting at us . . . at me! He wanted to shoot me and he shot Ernesto, instead. He could not tell us apart."

"I see what you mean," Clint said, "but you can't think about that now. It won't help to feel guilty."

"He is always getting me out of trouble, my brother," Eduardo said. "Maybe now I'll get him out of trouble, eh? Trouble I got him into in the first place."

"Maybe so, Eduardo," Clint said, "maybe so. We'll both try to get us all out of trouble."

"Right!" Eduardo agreed enthusiastically.

"Take this," Clint said, passing him the dead man's Navy Colt. "Can you use it?"

"I can use it," Eduardo assured Clint, tucking the gun into his belt.

"Go and get your uncle and Ana mounted up," Clint told him, "and then take the fourth horse for yourself."

"I said I would walk," Eduardo argued.

"We'll take turns, Eduardo," Clint said. "Do you know

the way to the river, or do we have to rely on your uncle in his condition?''

"I know the way," Eduardo said.

"Good, then you'll ride the point. I'll lead Ernesto's horse," Clint said.

"He is my brother," Eduardo said. "I should lead his horse.''

"You're going to lead us all, Eduardo," Clint said. "Lead us all to safety."

Eduardo studied Clint for a few moments, then nodded shortly and said, "All right. I'll get my uncle and Ana."

"We haven't much daylight left," Clint said, "and I want to get as far from here as we can. Will we reach the river sometime tomorrow?''

"If we could move fast, I would say yes," Eduardo said.

"We'll get an early start then, and travel until late," Clint said. "Maybe we can still make it."

"We will try," Eduardo said sagely.

"I'll get your brother, and we'll start," Clint said, putting his hand on Eduardo's shoulder. "We're in your hands now, Eduardo. It's your skill and courage that will help us now."

"And luck, Clint," Eduardo said. "Don't forget about the luck."

Chapter Seventeen

They started off with Eduardo in the lead, Ramirez and Ana in the middle, riding side by side, and Clint bringing up the rear, leading Ernesto's horse. After a few hours, they moved Ernesto up so that Eduardo was still leading, but walking his brother's horse. Clint, riding Eduardo's horse, was bringing up the rear. Their progress was much slower when this was the case, so Clint gave Eduardo more time with the horse than he did, and told him not to worry about his being able to keep up.

During one rest period Ana came back to where Clint was sitting and said, "We could ride double, if you like."

"Thanks, honey," Clint said, "but these animals wouldn't stand up under it."

"I could walk some," she said. "You are very tired."

"I'll be all right," he assured her, although she was right. His legs were especially getting tired, but he knew they had to keep going. Ernesto was only occasionally conscious now, and Clint could see by the sheen on his face and the glaze in his eyes that he was running a high fever.

During another rest stop he asked Eduardo, "Find out from your uncle if there will be medical supplies on the boat."

Eduardo asked the old man, and then came back.

"He thinks so," Eduardo said, "but he is not sure."

"How is he doing?"

"He will not complain, but he has pain, here," Eduardo said, touching his head.

"Headaches?"

"Yes."

"Any more dizziness?"

"Some," Eduardo answered, "but still he will not complain."

"I'll talk to Ana," Clint said. "She'll stay close to him, in case he starts to fall off his horse, or something."

"All right," Eduardo said. "My brother?"

"Talk to him," Clint said.

Eduardo nodded, walked over to where his brother was lying on the ground, and began talking to him in low tones that Clint could not hear.

"Is he going to die?" Ana asked, coming up behind him.

"I hope not, Ana," Clint said. "The wound itself isn't that bad, but there's a danger of infection if he doesn't get medical attention pretty soon."

"Isn't there something we can do?" she asked. "The bleeding continues."

"Yeah," Clint said. "It's not bad, but it is still bleeding. Maybe there is something we can do."

He walked over to where the brothers were talking and said, "Ernesto, I think there may be something that we can do to stop the bleeding."

"Yes?"

Clint went on to tell him what he was thinking of doing, and then left the decision to him and his brother. They talked it over between them, in Spanish, and then Eduardo looked at Clint and said, "We will go ahead."

"All right," Clint said.

He crouched down by Eduardo and removed a bullet from his gunbelt. Using a small knife, he pried the slug off the shell, exposing the 240 grains inside. He took out another bullet and told Ernesto, "Take this between your teeth."

Ernesto opened his mouth and Clint placed the bullet between his teeth.

"Expose the wound," Clint instructed Eduardo.

When the wound was exposed Clint sprinkled the gunpowder over it, and then told Eduardo, "Hold him tight."

With Eduardo holding his brother securely by the shoulders, Clint took a lucifer and fired it off his nail, then touched the flame to the powder covering Ernesto's wound. As the powder flared Ernesto's entire body jerked and he bit down tightly on the bullet between his teeth. Clint placed his hands on the boy's legs and held them firmly to the ground. Between them, he and Eduardo held the wounded man as still as they could until the powder burned out, and the wound was seared closed.

"Where did you learn to do such a thing?" Eduardo asked Clint later.

"I've seen many gunshot wounds, Eduardo," Clint said. "You learn things."

"I see that," Eduardo said. "I am learning many things since I have met you, Clint."

"I'm glad to be of help, Eduardo," Clint said. "Now I think we'd better get going. It's going to be dark soon. I hope we can make the river before then."

"If not," Eduardo said, "have no fear. I can find it in the dark."

"That'll do fine," Clint said, "as long as Sykes and his friends don't find us first."

"If they do," Eduardo said, holding up the rifle Clint had given him, "we will take care of them again, no?"

"I'd rather just avoid them, Eduardo," Clint said. "Learn that, too. Avoid trouble whenever you can. Now let's get going."

• • •

When darkness finally fell, they paused to discuss the prospects of traveling farther in the dark.

"We are not very far now," Eduardo insisted. "We will be there soon."

Clint looked around, and there was really no one else to consider. It was up to him and Eduardo, and this was Eduardo's country.

"All right," Clint agreed, "we'll go on."

An hour later they reached the Paraguay River and Clint could see Eduardo's wide, satisfied smile in the moonlight.

"Okay, Eduardo," he said, "okay. Good work."

"Courage, skill," Eduardo said happily, ticking them off his fingers, "and luck, eh?"

"And a boat," Clint said, "I hope."

Chapter Eighteen

The boat was larger than Clint had expected it to be, but then, so was the river. He had not expected a body of water large enough to accommodate a Mississippi riverboat, but there it was.

The woodburner had plenty of room for the five of them, but no room for the horses.

"We'll leave them behind," Ramirez said, and Clint was surprised at the strength in his voice.

The men on the boat were his, and it was as if having his own men there made him feel more in control.

"We must get underway," he said.

"Yes, Uncle," Eduardo said.

"Ana, help Señor Ramirez aboard," Clint said, realizing that although the old man sounded better, he wasn't. "Eduardo and I will bring Ernesto aboard."

Ramirez spoke in rapid Spanish to two of the men on board, and they hurried to the horses to take any supplies that might come in handy.

Together, Clint and Eduardo eased Ernesto off the horse as gently as they could and carried him on board. The boat had a cabin, and they carried him down there where he would stay with his uncle. Ana assigned herself to be nurse to both of them, although there proved to be no medical supplies on board. Clint's cauterization of the wound had proved effective, however. The bleeding had stopped, the fever had gone down, and the danger of infection seemed to have subsided.

"I will stay with them," Ana said.

"Fine."

"I do not need a woman—" Ramirez began to say, but he was cut off by Ana.

"Keep quiet," she said, and Ramirez lapsed into a shocked silence.

"I think she'll be able to handle him," Clint said to Eduardo. "Let's go outside."

They went out and saw two of the four man crew carrying supplies onto the boat.

"What do we do with the horses, Señor?" one of them asked Eduardo.

He looked at Clint, as if expecting the Gunsmith to answer the question, and when he didn't Eduardo said, "Let them go. They will find their way back, or become food for a jaguar."

Eduardo looked at Clint for confirmation, and the Gunsmith simply nodded.

The men went and released the horses, then jumped on board. In a few moments the boat was traveling downriver, and Eduardo said, "I suppose we will not have any more trouble with Mr. Sykes."

"I hope not," Clint said, but Eduardo noticed that his new friend did not look happy.

"You do not seem pleased," he commented.

"It's nothing," Clint said.

"Are you ill, or hurt?" Eduardo asked, showing concern.

"No, it's nothing like that," Clint said. He saw that Eduardo's concern was deepening, so he turned to the young man and said, "This is simply not my favorite mode of travel, Eduardo. I don't like boats."

"That is unfortunate," Eduardo said, "because we do not have a short trip ahead of us."

"Yeah," Clint said, touching the scar on his cheek, "I know that."

Chapter Nineteen

At first light Clint abandoned his fitful night's sleep and began studying the shoreline, looking for signs of trouble from Sykes, or anywhere else.

"Breakfast?" Eduardo asked him, coming up next to him.

"Just coffee," Clint said.

"What are you looking for?" Eduardo asked when he returned with the coffee.

"Anything I don't like," Clint said. "I just don't want to be surprised from shore."

"Shall I have a man watch the other side, then?"

Clint looked at Eduardo and said, "That's a very good idea, Eduardo."

The younger man beamed at the praise, and then went off to give the order to one of the crew men. While Clint was drinking his coffee Ana came up from below to stand next to him.

"Good morning," he said to her.

"Good morning, Clint," she said. She appeared well rested, in spite of having two men to look after.

"How are your patients?" he asked.

"They are fine," she answered. "Ernesto was able to sleep, and so was Señor Ramirez. He wants to rise, but each time he does he becomes dizzy."

"When we reach his ranch I hope we'll be able to get both of them some proper medical care."

"I have tried to keep them comfortable," she said in her own defense.

"You've done a marvelous job, Ana," he said.

"Then you are glad I am here?"

"I'm not unhappy," he said, choosing his words carefully, "but I would like to know what you were doing out here all alone yesterday."

She told him, then, about being in the barn when Sykes and the other man, Josh, were talking, and about how she had taken a horse to find him and warn him.

"That was a foolish thing to do, Ana," he scolded her, "but I appreciate the thought behind it. Thank you."

"I did not want to see you die," she said, simply, and he echoed the sentiment.

When he finished his coffee she asked, "Would you like me to get you some more?"

"Sure," he said, handing her the empty cup, "thanks."

She passed Eduardo on the way and smiled at him. When he came up next to Clint he was still looking back at her.

"She's very pretty, isn't she?" Clint asked.

"Beautiful," Eduardo said, and Clint could tell by the sound of his voice that he had been soundly smitten.

"Did you get someone set up on the other side?" he asked.

"What?" Eduardo said. "Oh, yes, I have a man keeping watch. When it is his turn to feed the woodburner, another man will take his place."

"That's good," Clint said.

Ana came back with Clint's coffee, again favoring Eduardo with a smile.

"Why don't you get Eduardo a cup, Ana?" Clint asked.

"Whatever you say, Clint," she replied, and went off to get it.

"She seems very fond of you," Eduardo said.

"Do you think so?"

"Oh, yes," Eduardo answered. "I, uh, wondered if you and, er, she . . ."

"What?"

The younger man was embarrassed, and Ana's appearance at that moment with his coffee only served to make it worse.

"Uh, thank you," he said to her.

"It is nothing," she said. She turned to Clint and said, "I will go down and see if Ernesto or Señor Ramirez will take any breakfast."

"It might be a good idea to get them to eat something," Clint said. "It will keep their strength up."

"I will see you later," she said, and vanished down below. Eduardo watched her until she was out of sight, then leaned over the side and watched the dirty river water go by.

"You wanted to ask me something?" Clint reminded him.

"It was nothing important," Eduardo assured him.

"A man's got something on his chest, he should get it off real quick before his chest caves in under the weight."

"I have nothing on my chest, Clint," Eduardo insisted. He sipped his coffee, then dumped the rest of it into the river. "I will check on our wood supply. Excuse me."

"Sure, Eduardo, sure," Clint said.

Initially, he had been amused by Eduardo's obvious interest in Ana, but now it began to bother him. If she continued to heap special attention on Clint, it might cause some friction between himself and Eduardo. He didn't need that extra problem.

Maybe sending her back on foot yesterday might not have been such a bad idea, after all.

They stopped along the way to stock up on wood, nighttime stops at villages along the shore. They didn't see anyone along the shore during the trip, let alone feel threatened. The trip was uneventful, and for Clint Adams that made it perfect.

"We are here," Eduardo announced, when they finally reached their destination.

"It's about time," Clint said. He had drunk a lot of coffee during the trip, but eaten very little. On a Mississippi paddleboat, at least he was able to eat, but here the traveling was done a lot closer to the water, and that didn't make it easy for him to swallow.

"I hope there'll be some horses here," Clint said.

"At the end of the dock," Eduardo said.

"Then let's get your brother and uncle up here," Clint said, "and get to your uncle's ranch. Can you send one of the men for a doctor?"

"Of course."

Eduardo spoke rapidly to one of the men, and then followed Clint below.

"I can walk," Ramirez was complaining as Eduardo descended.

"Sure, I know you can," Clint said, "but give the young lady something to do. Lean on her, anyway."

With one arm around her shoulders, Ana helped Ramirez up the steps while Clint and Eduardo together carried Ernesto up. The man Eduardo had sent to check on the horses was waiting for them, and said something Clint couldn't understand.

"The horses are at the end of the dock," Eduardo told Clint.

"Decent ones, I hope," Clint said. "All right, let's get to them, then. The quicker your brother gets medical attention, the better."

They hurried along the docks to the end, where half a dozen horses were being held by one man.

"It is not a long ride to the ranch," Eduardo said as they sat Ernesto astride one of the horses.

"Good," Clint said. "I'm hungry." Now that his feet were on firm ground again, the pangs of hunger had started clawing at his stomach.

He took the reins offered to him by the ranch hand who had been holding all of the horses and examined the animal. It was younger and much fitter than the animals they had ridden out of Bogotá. It was actually a fairly decent animal, but it still didn't compare to Duke, and it still wasn't what he would want underneath him while tracking the Devil Cat.

"You're still going to have to do better, Señor Ramirez," he said to himself as he wheeled the animal around to follow the others, "a lot better."

Chapter Twenty

When they arrived at the ranch house there was a flurry of activity. They were met by a group of men who carried Ernesto and Ramirez into the house, while others took charge of the horses and led them away.

Eduardo came up next to Clint and said, "I will have someone show you and Ana to your rooms."

Clint looked at the huge, rambling house and said, "I'll bet you've got plenty of rooms too."

"We have quite a few," Eduardo admitted.

He waved to an elderly woman and said, "Carmelita will show you where you can rest and bathe. Dinner will be served at eight. By then we should know of Ernesto and my uncle's conditions."

"That's fine," Clint said. "You've done quite a job of taking charge, Eduardo."

Eduardo looked embarrassed and said, "Someone has to, until my uncle is back on his feet and ready to take over again."

"I'm sure you'll do fine until then," Clint said. "He'll be very proud of you."

"That would be a change," Eduardo said, seriously.

He left and Clint and Ana followed the elderly woman, who was giving the barefooted Ana disapproving looks.

"I do not think she likes me," Ana whispered to Clint.

"Maybe she just doesn't like your feet," he suggested.

The girl looked down at her feet in confusion and asked, "What is wrong with my feet?"

Clint leaned closer and said, "I don't think they are clean enough for her."

"I cannot help that," the young girl said. "I do not own a pair of shoes."

"Well, we'll see what we can do about that," Clint promised. "We'll have to get me a good horse, and you a pair of shoes."

Chapter Twenty-One

After leaving Ana off at her room, Clint followed Carmelita down the hall where she ushered him into his room. He was impressed by its size, the comfort of the bed, and the fact that there was a connecting door to a room with a bathtub in it. As he examined the bathtub, another door opened and a young boy carrying a bucket of hot water entered, dumped the water into the tub, and then left, presumably to fetch another pail of water.

"Can't beat this," Clint muttered backing out of the room. A hot bath was a welcome thought after all of the traveling they had done since Bogotá. He unbuckled his gunbelt and laid it aside on the bed, then stripped to his underwear. Taking fresh clothes from his saddlebag, he picked up his gun again and reentered the bathroom. The tub was still several buckets of water away from being filled, so he grabbed a chair and sat down to remove his boots.

When the boy had properly filled the tub Clint passed him a South American coin, which the boy snatched from his hand with obvious relish. He bowed his thanks, and ran out.

Clint stripped off his underwear, pulled the chair over next to the tub, hung his gunbelt over the back, and then got into the tub. This time, there was no thought of being watched, and he simply lay back and allowed the hot water to bake off the sweat, grime and aches.

As the water began to turn tepid he picked up the soap, scrubbed off the remaining dirt and grime, and then got out of the tub and dried off. He carried the fresh clothing and gunbelt back into his room and dressed in there. That done, he walked over to the room's only window, pushed aside the curtain and looked out. His room overlooked the front of the house, and he could see Eduardo talking to a few men, one of whom seemed to be giving him an argument. Eduardo replied, waving his hands about and pointing to the house. Two of the men nodded and walked away, seemingly satisfied, but the third man stood his ground and said a few more words to Eduardo before he too walked away. He was a big man, somewhere in his thirties, and Clint assumed that he didn't like the idea of taking orders from the younger Eduardo. Could the man have been the foreman of the ranch? Maybe he'd find out the answer if he stopped looking out the window and went downstairs. It was starting to get dark, and he figured it was nearing dinnertime anyway.

He strapped on his gunbelt, hoping that his host would understand when he showed up for dinner wearing his gun. Like it or not, he was the Gunsmith, and it would be downright unhealthy for him to walk around without his iron strapped to his hip, even in another country.

When he went downstairs he saw Ramirez and Eduardo from the steps, deep in conversation. As he reached the bottom they both looked over at him and backed away from each other a few feet.

"Clint," Eduardo said.

"Are you happy with your room, Señor Adams?" Ramirez asked. The old man seemed steady on his feet, and back in control of himself again. Possibly the home surroundings had given him back the confidence he had been losing little by little since leaving.

"It's fine, thank you," Clint said. "I'm glad to see you on your feet and looking so well."

"I am still a little dizzy," Ramirez commented, "but on the whole I am feeling much better. The doctor feels there is no permanent damage."

"And Ernesto? How is he?"

"He's going to be fine," Eduardo said.

"The doctor indicated that you might have saved his life when you cauterized the wound," Ramirez added. "We are grateful to you."

"I'm just sorry I didn't have time to think of it sooner," Clint said.

"We were all a little busy at the time," Eduardo said.

"I will see if the cook is ready to serve dinner," Ramirez said. "Excuse me."

The old man left the room and Clint moved over closer to Eduardo.

"Were you arguing when I came down?" he asked the young man.

Eduardo smiled ironically and said, "Let's just say that Uncle was not as proud of me as you thought he might be."

"I don't understand."

"I do not either," Eduardo admitted.

"What was his beef?" Clint asked.

"His beef?" Eduardo asked, not understanding.

"His complaint," Clint explained. "I thought you did quite well running things."

"I suppose my uncle just wanted me to know that he was back to 'running things,' as you put it. I think perhaps we should go into dinner now."

"Who else will be at dinner?" Clint asked, following Eduardo from the room.

"My cousin will join us," Eduardo answered.

"Your cousin?" Clint asked. He knew that Ramirez had one dead son, and another who was supposedly "mad."

"Does he eat with the family, then?"

Eduardo frowned at the question, then said, "Oh, I understand. No, the cousin I am referring to is Uncle's daughter.''

"Daughter!" Clint said. "I didn't know he had a daughter. I thought he only had two sons."

"And a daughter," Eduardo said. "I believe you will be impressed by my cousin Juliana."

"When will I get to meet your other cousin, the one who saw the jaguar?"

"Alonzo," Eduardo said. "He stays upstairs in his room and never comes out. He remains calm as long as he stays in his room."

"I'm going to have to talk to him," Clint said.

"We know that," Eduardo said. "I'm sure my uncle will take you up to see him, after dinner."

"All right," Clint said.

"When will you want to start after the Devil Cat?" Eduardo asked.

"There's no sense in wasting time," Clint said. "I'd like to pick out a horse in the morning and get started."

"I want to go with you," Eduardo said.

"Eduardo—"

"My uncle will have no say in the matter," Eduardo said quickly as they approached the dining room. "It will be up to you—if you want me."

"Eduardo—"

"Shh," Eduardo said. "We will speak of it later."

As they approached Clint saw Ramirez seated at the head of the table, and no one else around. It was a large, wooden table about twelve feet long, but there were only four places set around it.

"I thought your cousin—"

"Juliana likes to make an entrance," Eduardo said, "especially when there is a guest in the house."

"I see."

"Please, Señor Adams," Ramirez invited, "take a seat.

Dinner is almost ready. We have only to wait for my daughter, Juliana.''

"So Eduardo told me," Clint said, taking the seat to Ramirez's left. Eduardo sat opposite his uncle, leaving the seat across from Clint for the young lady they were all waiting for. "I didn't know you had a daughter."

"It was not necessary for the terms of your employment," Ramirez said.

"I see."

At that moment Clint heard a rustling sound, like a woman's skin rubbing against silk, and Ramirez said, "Ah, my dear," and stood up.

Clint looked towards the entrance to the dining room and stood up. He was conscious of Eduardo watching his face, and smiling as his jaw dropped.

"Señor Adams," Ramirez said, "my daughter, Juliana."

Chapter Twenty-Two

Juliana Ramirez was a tall, regal, strikingly beautiful young woman, not at all what Clint had expected—though what he had expected, he didn't exactly know. No one had spoken of Juliana until moments earlier, and he guessed maybe he thought that the reason for that was that she was something less than remarkable.

He was wrong. She was very remarkable, indeed.

"Señor Adams," she said, inclining her head slightly.

"Miss Ramirez—"

"You may call me Juliana, Mr. Adams," she said in perfect English.

"Thank you," Clint said, "and I wish you would call me Clint."

"Thank you," she said. "I think I shall."

She moved towards her place, and Eduardo moved around the table to hold the chair for her.

"Thank you, Cousin," she said, seating herself delicately.

Now that she was seated directly across from him, Clint was free to study her, without seeming to stare.

Her hair was long and blonde, her skin the color of alabaster, her eyes blue, all of which confused Clint slightly. Ramirez had dark, leathery skin, brown eyes and black hair, yet this incredibly fair, lovely creature was his daughter.

She was wearing a high-necked gown which accentuated

the thrust of her full breasts, the trimness of her tiny waist, the bloom of her generous hips.

"My mother was born in your country," she said to Clint, "and she was as fair as I am, which is why you see such a contrast between my father and myself."

"Juliana," Ramirez said, "there is no need to inform Señor Adams of useless facts about our past."

"Facts pertaining to my mother are not so useless," Juliana said smoothly to her father.

At that moment, the cook entered with a large, steaming bowl and placed it in the center of the table. He was an elderly man who seemed barely strong enough to carry the load, but he set it down gently and said to Ramirez, "I will get the meat," and shuffled back to the kitchen.

"For your benefit," Ramirez said to Clint, "all of us who live in this house will speak English in your presence."

"I appreciate that," Clint said.

"Father does not want you to think that any of us are talking about you," she said, smiling, and then she said something to Eduardo in her native tongue that made him smile.

"Juliana!" Ramirez snapped.

She did not seem the least bit chastened by his tone, but fell silent, obediently.

"Uncle, Clint would like to get an early start in the morning," Eduardo said.

"We will have dinner, and then discuss the hunt," Ramirez said. "Eduardo, please, you will serve in the absence of . . . of others."

"Yes, Uncle."

Eduardo served the soup, and when the cook brought in the meat—venison, from what Clint could see—he carved and served it, as well. Vegetables came next, and last but not least, Eduardo poured the wine.

"I propose a toast," Juliana said, holding her glass aloft. Her father frowned at her, but she continued, undaunted. Eduardo's look was dubious, but he lifted his glass, and Clint followed.

"To Mr. Clint Adams, who has come to rid us of the Devil Cat," Juliana continued. "May the good Lord guide his aim, and make him luckier than others have been."

"Luck will have nothing to do with it," Eduardo assured her.

"What makes you say that, Cousin?"

"I have seen Clint shoot, Cousin," Eduardo said. "He shoots as if the Lord sits on his shoulder."

"In that case, perhaps we should toast something else entirely," Juliana Ramirez said.

Clint raised his glass again and said, "I'll propose a toast to your beauty, then."

"How gallant," Juliana replied.

"You are easily the loveliest creature I've seen since my arrival in South America."

"I believe you mean that, Mr. Adams . . . I mean, Clint," she said.

"I do . . . Juliana."

"Well, in that case . . . ." she said, and sipped at her wine, not taking her eyes from his.

Eduardo shrugged, drank half of his own wine, and began to eat.

Chapter Twenty-Three

After dinner Ramirez stood up and said, "Juliana, you must excuse us. Mr. Adams, Eduardo and I will be going into the study to talk."

Juliana stared at her father and for a moment Clint thought that she was going to argue, but then she looked away from him to Clint and said, "Clint, if you need any help, please let me know." She stood up and said, "I'm the best shot in the country."

The three men stood up and watched her as she walked out of the room, and Clint let out a breath, as if he had been holding it ever since she entered the room.

"Gentlemen," Ramirez said, "please accompany me."

Ramirez preceded them out of the room, and they followed him to the study.

"Eduardo, please pour the sherry," Ramirez said, closing the door.

"Yes, Uncle."

"Mr. Adams," Ramirez said, "would you like a cigar?"

"Yes, thank you," Clint said. He smoked only rarely, but he had the feeling that any cigar Ramirez offered was one not to be missed.

He was right.

As he lit it and drew in the smoke, Ramirez said, "We grow and cure this tobacco ourselves."

"It's excellent."

Eduardo came over and handed Clint a snifter of sherry. It too was excellent.

"Shall we be seated?"

Ramirez sat, and Eduardo and Clint followed his example.

"You wish to get started in the morning, señor?" Ramirez asked.

"Yes."

"That is good," the old man said. "The sooner you rid us of this curse, the better. However, there are members of our alliance who would like to meet you. Do you object to this?"

"Not unless it delays me."

"It will not," Ramirez assured him. "They will be here within the hour."

"I see," Clint said. "Would you like to tell me what this meeting is about?"

"They simply wish to see what they have purchased with their money," Ramirez said.

"I hope they don't expect any trick shooting," Clint remarked, not sure he liked the idea of being put on display.

"I am sure that simply speaking with you will be satisfactory to them."

"I hope so," Clint said. He stood up and said, "If you don't mind, I'll go for a walk outside before they arrive, maybe check out your stock."

"Feel free," Ramirez said.

Eduardo stood up, as if to accompany him, but his uncle said, "You will stay with me please, Eduardo? We must finish our discussion."

Although it was said in the form of a request, Clint felt it was much more than that, and that Eduardo was responding to it as such.

"I'll see you both later," Clint said.

"My foreman has instructions to cooperate with you fully," Ramirez said. "You may have any horse on the grounds."

Clint nodded and left the room. He remembered the last time someone had said that to him, when he needed a horse to use while searching for Duke, who had been snatched. On that occasion, he had come up with a white horse named Lancelot, who was almost Duke's equal.

He did not expect to be as lucky this time.

Chapter Twenty-Four

When Clint walked outside he found a clear, pleasant night with a sky full of stars. He drew deeply on the cigar, then stepped off the porch and started toward the stables.

There was very little activity at that time of the evening, but as he approached the barn he could see a light inside, and hear voices. When he entered he saw a circle of five men seated on the ground, and they were playing cards. When he entered, they all looked up at him tensely, then relaxed when they saw that he wasn't Ramirez, or possibly the foreman—unless the foreman was also playing . . . which he was.

The man he had seen arguing with Eduardo got up from the circle, said something to the other men, and then approached Clint.

"Señor Adams?" he asked.

"That's right."

"You have come to look at the horses?"

"Yes."

The man didn't look happy about it, but he said, "I am to give you every cooperation."

"I'd appreciate it."

"This way."

They walked past the card players towards the back of the huge barn.

"How many horses do you have here?" Clint asked.

"Many" was the answer he got.

"I hope you have some better than those that were sent to the dock for us."

The man stopped and looked back at Clint with a blank expression on his face. Clint revised his earlier guess at the man's age, seeing now that he was in his early forties. He was a big man, who seemed to have a perpetually dour look on his face.

"We have the finest horses in the country," the man said, then turned and continued on.

That statement did not do much to reassure Clint.

They finally reached the rear portion of what was certainly the longest barn Clint had ever been in, and the foreman pointed to the rows of stalls on each side.

"Back here we have our better horses," the man said. "It would save you time to start with these."

"I see," Clint said. "Thanks for being so helpful."

"It is my job."

"What's your name?"

"Tolomeo," the man said, giving no indication as to whether it was his first or last name.

"I'll tell Señor Ramirez that you were extremely helpful," Clint said.

The man executed a slight bow, which seemed odd from a man his size, and then turned and walked back towards the front of the barn. Clint had a feeling he was going to either break up the game, or move it.

Clint approached the stalls and began examining the horses. Tolomeo appeared to have been right. These animals were much better looking than any others Clint had seen so far, and would have to be the best Ramirez could offer. They were young, strong and healthy, and Clint was able to pick out two or three that he wouldn't have minded riding. There were no Dukes—or Lancelots—in the bunch, but Clint wouldn't have been ashamed to ride any one of the few he approved of.

As Clint walked back towards the front of the barn the men who had been playing cards were gone, and so was Tolomeo. There was, however, someone waiting there for him, leaning against the barn wall, arms folded.

It was Juliana Ramirez.

Chapter Twenty-Five

"Good evening," he said, stopping a few feet from her.

"Any luck?" she asked.

"With the horses?" he asked. "I saw a few I wouldn't be ashamed to ride."

"Well, good," she said. "I wouldn't want the lack of a good mount to delay your hunt."

"Was that the truth," he asked, "about you being the best shot on the ranch?"

"I said in the country," she said, "and I don't lie."

"No, I don't suppose you do," he said.

"Your little friend didn't join us for dinner," she observed.

"Oh, you mean Ana?" Clint asked. "I wondered about that myself."

"She preferred to eat in Ernesto's room, while looking after him."

"That's good."

"That doesn't bother you?" Juliana asked. She crossed one leg in front of the other, scratching the toe of one boot with the heel of another. She had changed from her gown into riding clothes. "Make you jealous, I mean?"

"Why should it?"

She shrugged and said, "I don't know." She pushed away from the wall and asked, "Are you going back to the house?"

He nodded. "Your father has arranged to put me on display for the other members of his Alliance."

"Yes, they will want to meet you."

"What are you doing out here?"

She shrugged again and said, "I just felt like taking a walk. Do you mind if I walk back with you?"

"Not at all."

They left the barn together, and Clint realized for the first time how tall Juliana was. In her boot heels she was almost as tall as he was, and she walked so close to him that every few steps her shoulder brushed his.

"Will you be taking someone with you tomorrow?" she asked.

"I don't know," he replied, recalling what Eduardo had said earlier.

"Do you usually take someone with you when you hunt?"

He laughed shortly and said, "In spite of what you've heard, Juliana, hunting is not my profession."

"What about your shooting?" she asked. "Was Eduardo right about that?"

"That I have God sitting on my shoulder?" he asked. "I wouldn't go quite that far. I think God has a lot better places to spend his time."

"You do shoot well, though, don't you?"

He looked at her, grinned, and said, "Yes, I shoot quite well, Juliana."

"I'd like to see you shoot."

"Seems like we're getting back to the original question," Clint said.

"I know Eduardo wants to go with you," she said, "but you would do better to take me."

"I would do better to go alone," Clint said, "then I would have no one to worry about but myself."

"You wouldn't have to worry about me, Mr. Clint

Adams," she said, stiffening her shoulders. "I can take care of myself."

"I'm sure you can," Clint said.

"Then you'll take me with you?"

"I didn't say that."

"You didn't say no, either," she pointed out. "Do you usually tease your women this way?"

He stopped walking and turned his head to look at her. "You're not my woman."

"No," she replied, putting a hand on his chest, "but I could be."

She kissed him then, but before it could go too far he pulled his head away and stared into her beautiful eyes.

"You'd go this far just to hunt that cat with me?" he asked.

"That's not the only reason," she said. "You're not an unattractive man, you know."

"That's kind of you," he said, taking her hand and removing it from his chest, "but why don't we save this for another time, when we can both be sure what our reasons are?"

She pulled her hand from his grasp and her eyes flashed with anger. She was not used to being rebuffed by a man and didn't like the feeling.

"They are waiting for you inside," she said. "Go in and do your tricks for them, Mr. Adams. You will not find an appreciative audience out here."

"I wasn't looking for one, Miss Ramirez," he said, and she turned and stalked away from him to the house. Clint followed the angry sway of her fine hips and buttocks inside the tight jeans, then shook his head and followed in her wake.

Chapter Twenty-Six

When Clint entered the house he found Eduardo standing in the hall at the foot of the steps, glancing up. When he heard Clint he turned around and approached him.

"Did you talk with Juliana outside?" he asked.

"I did."

"What did you say to make her so angry?"

"I think it was 'No,' " Clint said. "Where are your uncle and the others?"

"In the study. I was coming to look for you."

"Well, you found me," Clint said. "Lead the way."

He followed Eduardo to the study door, where he knocked twice and opened the door.

"Mr. Adams, Uncle," he said, allowing Clint to precede him into the room, and then closing the door behind them.

"Ah, Mr. Adams," Ramirez said, rising from his chair. "Please, come and meet my . . . compatriots."

There were four other men in the room, and all were of a comparable age with Ramirez. The youngest may have been in his fifties, and all looked well fed and prosperous. Ramirez rattled off their names, but Clint paid little attention to the introductions. As far as he was concerned, he had been hired by Ramirez, and would report his progress to him. Let him worry about the others.

The men frankly studied Clint, then began to speak to each other in their own language.

"Gentlemen," Ramirez said, interrupting them. "I have assured Mr. Adams that only English would be spoken in his presence. It would be rude to do otherwise."

All four men looked at Ramirez, then at each other before nodding their heads.

"Mr. Adams," one man said in heavily accented English, "we are . . . pleased that you have accepted our offer to hunt the . . . Devil Cat." He pronounced the word *cat* as if it were *cot*, and paused frequently over the unfamiliar language.

"I was pleased to accept," Clint said, "but assuming you gentlemen aren't expecting parlor tricks, I don't see what this meeting will accomplish. I'd like to turn in so I can get an early start in the morning."

"Parlor . . . tricks?" the man who had spoken previously said, looking at Ramirez. He pronounced *tricks* as *treecks*.

"I can explain," Ramirez said, looking at Clint.

"In your own tongue, as well," Clint said, "because I am leaving. Good night, gentlemen."

As he turned to leave all of the men in the room began speaking at once. He was almost to the stairs when Eduardo came up behind him, calling his name.

"Clint—"

"Yes?"

"You certainly got their . . . their—what do you say?— backs up?"

"Right," Clint said. "A small price to pay for getting rid of that cat, isn't it?"

"I agree," Eduardo said. "My uncle feels that it will be important for you to have a guide, someone who knows the country. Who will you—"

"Tell your uncle I'll take you," Clint said, "and no one else."

"Me?" Eduardo said happily. "But that is wonderful—"

"You'd better turn in too, Eduardo. I want to start out early," Clint said, interrupting.

"There is one other thing."

"What's that?"

Eduardo came up the steps until he was one step below Clint and said, "My uncle wishes me to take you upstairs to see Alonzo."

"Now?" Clint asked.

"Yes, unless you would rather do it in the morning?"

"No," Clint said. "I don't want any delays at all in the morning. You'd better take me to him."

Eduardo nodded, passed Clint on the steps, and then led the way. When they reached the upper level they turned away from the direction of Clint's room and walked all the way to the end of the hall.

"He is here," Eduardo said. "We must enter gently."

"Go ahead," Clint said, impatient to speak to the only man who had seen this Devil Cat and lived.

"You must speak softly," Eduardo warned, "and not make any sudden movement with your hands. He frightens easily, and if he becomes too frightened he will not be able to speak."

"I'll remember," Clint said, clasping his hands together in front of him as a reminder.

"All right," Eduardo said. He knocked so gently on the door that Clint barely heard it, then turned the door knob and swung it open slowly.

"Lonzo," he called softly, "Lonzo, I have brought you a visitor."

Chapter Twenty-Seven

Clint followed Eduardo into the darkened room, being as light on his feet as he could. There was a musty smell in the room which made him think that there had not been an open window in that room for some time.

"Lonzo," Eduardo called again.

"Here," a voice called, so softly as to be almost unheard, yet in that one word Clint heard many things, the most outstanding of which was fear.

"I have brought someone to see you," Eduardo said.

"Who is it?"

"A friend," Eduardo said. "His name is Clint. May we turn up the lamp?"

There was hesitation, and then the voice said, "Yes, all right."

Eduardo put his hand on Clint's shoulder, as if to remind him not to move, and then walked to a lamp and lit it. He kept the flame low, and there was just barely enough light for Clint to see the man on the bed.

He felt as if he were looking at a younger, dark-haired version of the old man. Alonzo Ramirez was sitting up in bed, with his back against the headboard, and the look on his face was wary, and afraid. His eyes darted around the room like those of a trapped animal trying to find its pursuer.

"There is only us here, Alonzo," Eduardo assured him.

Alonzo looked at Eduardo, then flicked his eyes to Clint, who could see him visibly shrink away from the stranger in the room.

"Who is he?" Alonzo demanded. "What does he want?"

"His name is Clint, Lonzo," Eduardo said, approaching his cousin. He sat on the bed and Alonzo shrank away from him as well. "It's all right," Eduardo said, reaching his hand out to his cousin, "he's come here to kill the cat."

Clint expected the man on the bed to react violently to his counsin's announcement, but was surprised when Alonzo did not react at all.

"Alonzo," Eduardo said, "did you hear me?"

"I heard you," the other man said. "He has come to kill the Devil Cat."

"Yes."

"Good."

Eduardo looked at Clint through puzzled eyes. He too had expected a totally different reaction from his cousin.

"He needs your help, Alonzo," Eduardo said.

Alonzo looked directly at Clint and asked, "What can I do?"

"You're the only man who has seen the cat," Clint said, speaking softly. "Can you tell me anything about the animal?"

"Yes," Alonzo said, and his eyes seemed to turn inward, as if they were examining a memory. "He is evil."

Eduardo started to speak, but Clint waved a hand to keep him quiet.

"Go on," he said, gently.

"Evil," Alonzo went on, as if he hadn't heard, "and huge. I have never seen a jaguar such a size. He leapt upon my brother—" he said, then looked at Eduardo and said, "Duardo, you know what a big man Carlito was."

"I know," Eduardo said.

"The cat, he was too large for my brother," Alonzo said, "he just knocked him down and . . . and . . ."

At that point Alonzo's eyes began to widen, as if he was seeing it all again, and his breathing began to accelerate.

"He knocked him down and began clawing," he said, his voice rising, "and tearing at him with his teeth . . ."

"Eduardo," Clint said, warningly. Alonzo was about to go out of control, and Clint wanted to head that off.

"Easy, Alonzo—" Eduardo said, but his cousin didn't seem to hear him.

"He tore his throat out—" Alonzo shrieked, and his body began to tremble.

"What are you doing?" Juliana shouted from the doorway. Clint turned and watched as she rushed to her brother's bedside.

"You're making him see it all over again."

"Juliana—" Eduardo started.

"Get out," she shouted, "both of you get out!"

"Juliana," Alonzo shouted, "I can see him—"

"Alonzo, my brother—" she said, cradling his head in her arms. "Shh, my brother, it is all right." After that she began to speak in Spanish, and Clint waved at Eduardo to leave with him.

Out in the hall Clint said, "I'm sorry about that."

"I thought he was all right," Eduardo said, "and then all of a sudden—"

"It was my fault," Clint told him. "Look, you better get some sleep. We have to go hunting in the morning."

"Yes," Eduardo said, "right." He looked back at the door to Alonzo's room, which was ajar, then reached back and pulled it shut.

"You are still coming with me in the morning, aren't you, Eduardo?" Clint asked.

"Yes," Eduardo said, tearing his eyes away from the door

to his cousin's room. "Oh, yes, Clint, I am definitely coming with you."

"All right, then," Clint said. "I'll meet you at the barn at first light."

"Shall I have horses saddled for us?"

"No," Clint said, "I'll saddle my own horse, but you can have a packhorse loaded up for us. We don't know how long we're going to be out there."

"Of course."

They started down the hall and Clint could see that Eduardo had been deeply affected by what had happened with his cousin.

"Eduardo, maybe you'd better stay—"

"No!" Eduardo snapped. "Clint, I will be with you tomorrow, have no fear."

He walked to the door to his own room, turned and said, "Good night, Clint," and went inside, almost slamming the door behind him.

Clint stared at the door, and repeated, "Sure, have no fear."

He looked down the hall towards the room where a man was being consumed by fear, and then continued down the hall to his own room.

Chapter Twenty-Eight

The moment he entered his room he knew he wasn't alone.

"Hello," he called out.

"Clint—" a voice called out sleepily.

"Ana," he said.

"Yes."

He walked to the wall lamp and turned up the flame. Ana sat up in his bed, sleepily rubbing her eyes like a little girl.

"What are you doing here?" he asked.

"Waiting for you," she said. "I let myself in, and then I guess I fell asleep."

"That's what I want to do," he said, unstrapping his gun.

"You are not happy that I am here?"

"No, Ana, I am not," he replied. He really didn't feel like having a woman in his bed right now, and even if he did he surprised himself a bit by thinking that it wouldn't be Ana, it would be Juliana.

Ana threw back the covers and revealed herself to be wearing a nightshirt that someone had given her. Clint was glad she wasn't naked because he was, after all, only human.

"I will go," she said, dropping her chin to her chest, another little girl gesture.

"Don't be sad," he said, "or angry. I have to get an early start in the morning, and I must get some sleep."

"You will go hunting for the Devil Cat?" she asked.

"Someone told you about that?"

She nodded and said, "Ernesto."

"I see. How is he?"

"He is much better. Tomorrow he will get out of bed."

"That's great."

They stood there awkwardly for a few moments, and then Ana said, "I will go back to my room."

"That's a good idea, Ana."

She looked up at him with her big brown eyes and said, "Will I see you in the morning before you leave?"

"That depends on you," he said. "I'll be getting up pretty early."

"I will be up," she promised, "to wish you luck."

"Thanks," he said.

She smiled, looked longingly at his bed, and then said, "Good night, Clint."

"Good night, Ana."

She quietly let herself out of the room, and he sat down on the bed to remove his boots. He had just pulled off the second one when the door to his room burst open.

"Juliana," he said, surprised.

She glared at him, started to speak and then stopped long enough to shut the door behind her.

"What did you think you were doing?" she demanded, angrily planting her hands on her hips.

"Juliana, I'm sorry if I upset your brother—" he said, standing up with his boot still in his hand.

"Upset him?" she asked. "You terrified him all over again, made him see our brother being torn to pieces—"

"Juliana!" he snapped. "Calm down."

She glared at him, breathing angrily through her nose and she was more beautiful than she had been at dinner, with her gown and make up.

"I didn't mean to get your brother all riled up," he said. "I would think that you'd want me to do whatever I could to bag that cat."

"If you had bothered to ask me, I would have told you that there was nothing Alonzo could tell you."

"Your father said—"

"My father!" she said in disgust. She strode angrily around the room, hands still firmly planted on her hips, but balled into tight fists now.

"Juliana—"

"My father," she said, whirling on him, "has not been up to that room to see his son since they brought Alonzo back with Carlito's body."

Clint frowned and said, "Why?"

"I don't know," she said, and there was helplessness in her voice. "Maybe he blames Alonzo for our brother's death."

"Why should he do that?"

She dropped her hands to her sides now, but her hands were still balled up into fists.

"Alonzo's rifle had not been fired," she said. "A man like my father would turn something like that into a sign of cowardice."

Clint suddenly became aware of the fact that he was still holding his boot in his hand and allowed it to drop to the floor.

"Your father hasn't struck me as the most understanding man in the world," he said, "but to hold that against your brother—I mean, not to want to see him again—"

"He also forbids Alonzo to leave that room," she added, "not that he wants to. He is convinced that the Devil Cat is waiting out in the hall for him."

Clint looked over at the night table next to his bed, upon which sat a decanter of wine. He assumed there was a similar decanter in each room in the house.

"Would you care for a glass of wine?" he asked.

She looked at the decanter, then said, "Yes, I would."

He walked to the table and poured two glasses of wine, and

handed Juliana one. She drank half of it down, then took a long, shuddering breath.

"Juliana," he said, "why don't you just take your brother away?" he asked.

She looked at him and said, "This is our home."

Some home, he thought, but he kept it to himself.

"I saw your little friend leave just before I came in," she said.

"She was waiting here for me," he said.

"Did you enjoy her?"

"I sent her away," he said.

"Really?" she asked. "I find that hard to believe. Doesn't she please you?"

"She's lovely," he said, "I just wasn't in the mood."

She finished her wine and extended the glass. "More, please."

He poured her more and she accepted the glass back.

"I don't know whether or not to believe you," she said.

"I really don't care what you believe," he replied.

"I'm still angry with you from before, you know," she told him.

"Juliana," he said, "I'm really very tired and I need to get some rest before morning. Would you finish your drink and then leave?"

He turned his back on her and began to remove his shirt, and before he realized what was happening she was upon him, hammering at his back with her fists.

"You bastard!" was one of the things she was shouting at him, but it was the only thing that was in English, so it was all he was able to understand.

"Juliana—" he said, staggering under her weight. "Goddamn it, Juliana!"

"Bastard!" she spat again.

He had been trying to get her away from him without too

much force, but now he simply turned, put his hand against her chest, and shoved her away. She staggered backward and fell on her behind heavily, but was up and at him again in a flash.

"What's wrong with you?" he asked, grabbing for her wrists before she could land any more punches.

"Damn you!" she shouted at him. "I'm angry, and I'm frustrated, and you had the nerve . . . to say no . . ." She continued trying to pull free of him, and then she began to kick. He held her wrists tightly, spun her around and pushed her down onto the bed, landing on top of her, pinning her arms to the mattress.

"Calm down—"

"Damn you, Clint," she cried out, "I've either got to beat on someone . . . or love someone."

She stared into his eyes and suddenly stopped struggling. He became acutely aware of her as a woman then, and of the fact that he was on top of her, in bed. Her firm breasts were rising and falling rapidly and her blouse had been torn half open during their struggle, revealing the tops of her creamy breasts.

"Clint—" she whispered. She reached for him with her mouth, picking her head up off the mattress, and he leaned down to kiss her.

Her tongue thrust into his mouth and he released her wrists so that he could open her blouse the rest of the way and palm her breasts. She moaned as her nipples swelled beneath his palms, and she pushed her hands inside of his shirt and slid it off of him.

"Clint, oh, Clint—" she murmured as he pressed his lips to the pulse in her neck.

"You've got a lot of violence inside of you," he said to her, "a lot of anger, and resentment."

"Yes," she said, "yes."

He stared down at her lovely face, flushed now with desire and said, ''Well, we'll just see if we can't find a less harmful way for you to let it out.''

Chapter Twenty-Nine

Clint undressed Juliana first, exciting her even more with his hands while he slipped her clothes from her alabaster body. She watched him then, anxiously, as he undressed himself, and then climbed back onto the bed with her.

"Clint—"

"Shh," he said, running his fingertips over her body, tweaking her nipples, sliding one hand between her legs, kissing and sucking her nipples while dipping first one finger, and then a second into the steaming depths of her while she moaned and raised her hips off the bed to meet the pressure of his hand.

"Oh damn," she said, "stop fooling around."

With surprising strength she pushed him over so she could reverse their positions. Grasping his long erection in both hands she hastily mounted him and guided him inside of her, until she was grinding herself against him, with the length of him buried inside of her.

"Oh, God—" she moaned and began to rotate her hips back and forth.

He reached up to grasp her full breasts and bring her down to where he could squeeze them together and suck both of her nipples at one time. The combined sensations seemed to trigger something inside of her and all of that pent-up anger and violence spilled out.

She began to ride him wildly, up and down, back and

forth, grinding herself against him, trying to drive him deeper and deeper inside of him. Clint, feeling as if he were going to burst any moment, gritted his teeth and held back, because he knew she needed this release.

"Oh God, yes," she cried out, "yes, damn it, yes . . ."

She put her palms against his chest and then began to dig her nails into him as her body started to tremble.

"Oh, yes, now," she said, "do it now . . ."

He was glad to hear those words, because he couldn't have held back much longer. He exploded inside of her, and he could feel her insides grasping him, taking all he had to offer and sucking even more from him.

"Oh, yes . . ." she said. She collapsed on top of him, licking perspiration from his neck and shoulders. "Um," she murmured against his throat, "I needed that, I needed that very badly."

She relaxed, slid off of him and lay down beside him. She took a deep breath, held it, and let it out very slowly.

Clint propped himself up on one elbow and looked down at her. Her skin was damp with perspiration, and there were beads of it on her upper lip, her forehead, and in the valley between her full breasts. He leaned over and ran his tongue along that valley, collecting every drop.

"Ooh," she said, placing one hand on the back of his head as he circled her nipples with his tongue.

"How do you feel?" he asked.

"Wonderful," she said, rubbing the back of his neck as he looked down at her. She stretched then, putting both hands over her head, flattening her breasts out and spreading her legs. "I feel wonderful," she said again.

"Good," he said, "because I have to get some sleep, or I'm liable to end up the hunted instead of the hunter."

"Yes," she said, looking at him, "I have to get some sleep, too."

"Oh?" he said suspiciously. "Why?"

She sat up and said, "Because I'm going with you."

She stood up and started to get dressed, and he sat up and said, "Now wait a minute—"

"You're not going to change my mind," she said, slipping into her pants.

"Just because we—"

"If you don't let me ride with you, I'll ride along behind you," she told him. "How would you feel if that cat got me because you wouldn't let me ride with you?"

"Juliana, I'm taking Eduardo with me—"

"Ha," she said, buttoning her blouse, "a lot of good he'll do you. He's a terrible shot."

"Juliana, damn it—"

Dressed, she leaned over him and kissed him on the mouth, fleetingly.

"I'll see you in the morning, Clint," she said, and headed for the door.

"You know, Juliana," he said, helplessly, "you're really something."

She opened the door, looked back at him, and said, "You know, so are you," and shut the door behind her.

Exhausted from the session with Juliana, Clint fell off to sleep as soon as he got over the frustration she had caused him with her announcement that she was going with him, one way or the other, whether he liked it or not.

He dreamed that he was being chased by a big jaguar with Juliana riding on its back saying, "See? I told you you would be sorry."

He awoke just before first light and decided against taking a bath. He didn't want to feel too comfortable at the start of the day, for fear that it might lull him into a false sense of security. As soon as they rode away from the ranch he wanted to feel as if there were a jaguar behind every bush and hiding in every tree. He wanted to be ready for this Devil Cat, wherever it came from and whenever it came.

He got up and dressed quickly, wondering if Juliana might not oversleep. She must have been as exhausted as he had been, maybe more. She had released a lot of pent-up emotions last night, and that usually left a person drained, both emotionally and physically.

One look out the window after he was dressed shot that theory all to hell. He saw Juliana walking briskly to the barn, ahead of him, and probably ahead of her cousin, as well. From the spring in her step, she was feeling pretty energetic, too.

Shaking his head he strapped on his gun, tucked the New Line Colt inside his shirt, and picked up his Springfield.

The hunt was just about to start.

Chapter Thirty

When Clint got to the barn Juliana had already saddled a horse for herself. It was one of the horses he had picked out the night before.

"Good morning," she greeted, cheerfully.

He put his rifle down and stared at her.

"Eduardo was just here," she said. "He took a horse around back to load up with supplies."

"Good," he said. "I don't suppose I can talk you out of this, this morning."

She gave him a wry grin and said, "My dear, if you couldn't talk me out of it last night, what makes you think you will be able to this morning?"

"You have a good point there," he said. "I'm going to saddle a horse."

"Take the sorrel in the last stall," she said. "He's the best we've got. I left him for you."

"Thank you."

He walked to the rear of the barn, glanced once at the sorrel, and then began to saddle the dun in the stall next to it.

When he walked the horse outside Juliana turned and looked at him in surprise.

"I left the sorrel for Eduardo," he explained. Actually, he had simply preferred the dun to the sorrel. It looked surefooted and he didn't think it would spook unnecessarily.

139

When the animal got nervous, the chances were good it would mean that he had picked up the cat's scent.

They heard footsteps approaching and turned to find Ramirez walking towards them.

"Good morning, Father," Juliana said, formally.

He nodded at her, then looked at Clint.

"You are taking my daughter with you?"

"It isn't by choice, I assure you, señor," Clint said, exchanging glances with Juliana.

"I told him that if he did not let me ride along with him, I would follow him."

"She'll be safer with us," Clint added.

"With us?" Ramirez asked, frowning.

Clint looked past him and Ramirez turned to see Eduardo leading a supply laden horse.

"You better saddle up," he told the younger man as he reached them. "Take the sorrel."

Eduardo nodded, exchanged neutral looks with his uncle, and then went into the barn.

"If you have Juliana, why are you taking Eduardo?" Ramirez asked. "My daughter knows this country."

Clint shrugged and said, "Eduardo is the one I asked to come along. Juliana is coming of her own accord. I want her to feel free to turn back at any time."

"I won't turn back," she said, forcefully.

"I don't expect you to," Clint said, truthfully, "but feel free to at any time."

Eduardo came out walking the sorrel and Clint said, "I guess we're ready."

He mounted the dun and gathered up the reins of the packhorse. He rode over to where Juliana had mounted her bay and handed her the reins. She stared at him.

"If you're going to come along, you'll have to make yourself useful," he explained. "Eduardo is my guide, and I need my hands free to go for my gun at any time. That leaves you to lead the packhorse."

Holding the animal's reins in her hand she asked, "And who would lead it if I stayed behind?"

He grinned at her and said, "Stay behind and find out."

Wheeling his horse around without waiting for a response he said to Eduardo, "Lead the way."

Ramirez stood silently by, watching them ride out, and Clint wondered why he hadn't bothered to wish them good luck. Maybe he was afraid that one of his family members would interpret it as a show of emotion.

We couldn't have that, the Gunsmith thought, *could we?*

Raphael Ramirez watched the three riders until they were out of sight, then turned and looked back at his house. From where he stood, he could see the window to Alonzo's room. Perhaps, he thought, if the man known as the Gunsmith were to truly hunt and kill the Devil Cat, perhaps he would then have one son back.

Once the devil was dead, things would be different, wouldn't they?

Chapter Thirty-One

Much of the first half of that first day, they traveled single file, which was not conducive to conversation.

"Pull up, Eduardo," Clint called. He stopped, and Juliana caught up to him.

"What's wrong?" she asked.

"Nothing," he answered, "I just want to give these animals a rest."

Eduardo rode back to where they were and they all dismounted and allowed the horses to graze.

"Where do you want to start?" Eduardo asked Clint. "We did not discuss this."

"Well, where were you taking us?" Clint asked.

"To the place where the Devil Cat killed Carlito," Eduardo answered.

"That's where I want to start," Clint said. "How far are we from there, now?"

"An hour, perhaps a little more," Eduardo said.

"All right. We'll give the horses a few minutes, and then go on. Juliana, check the packhorse, make sure everything is secure."

She threw him a resentful look, but went off and did what he said.

Clint turned to Eduardo and said, "Did you talk to your uncle about incidents with the cat since you left South America?"

"No one was killed, but a few of the other ranches lost some livestock."

"Has the cat been hitting any one particular ranch more than others?"

"Ours, I think," Eduardo said. "My uncle is beginning to feel that it is a curse someone has wished upon us."

"That's nonsense."

"Perhaps," Eduardo said, "but consider that my uncle has lost two sons, and then you might understand why he feels this way."

"He's lost one son, that I can see," Clint said. "He could get the other one back if he wanted to."

Eduardo frowned at Clint, then threw a glance towards Juliana.

"We talked," Clint admitted, looking over at the girl.

"Perhaps too much."

"Perhaps not enough," Clint said. "I don't like working in the dark, Eduardo."

"There were things my uncle felt you did not need to know in order to hunt the cat."

"It seems to me that your uncle has been wrong about many things," Clint said. "You, for one."

"Me?"

"You seem able to handle more responsibility than he seems willing to give you."

"Ernesto is the responsible one," Eduardo said.

"Don't doubt yourself just because others do, Eduardo," Clint said. "If I didn't think you capable, I wouldn't have taken you with me."

"I appreciate it," Eduardo assured him. "I would like very much to avenge my cousin's death."

"Just don't get foolish on me," Clint said. "If we come across this cat, let me handle it."

"And what of Juliana?" Eduardo asked. "It was her

brother who was killed. Her thirst for vengeance must surely be stronger than my own."

"I'll tell her the same thing," Clint said.

He left Eduardo and walked over to where Juliana was checking the load on the packhorse.

"Everything seems secure," she told him.

"Good."

She leaned on the horse and asked, "Do you intend to continue to give me the menial tasks to do?"

"Somebody's got to do them," he said.

"As long as I get a shot at that devil," she said, "I will gladly do them. You won't get me to go back that easily."

"I told you before, Juliana," Clint said, "I'm not trying to force you into going back. However, I'll tell you the same thing I told Eduardo. Don't try to play hero on me. When we come across that cat, I get first shot at him. That's what I'm being paid for."

"By my father," she reminded him. "That should also mean that you're working for me."

"I'm working for the alliance," Clint said, "and as long as you're along, you are working for me. Let's get that straight right now, or you can go off on your own."

"You wouldn't dare," she said, eyes flashing.

"Try me," he invited.

They locked eyes for a few moments, and then Juliana allowed hers to slide away. "As long as we get him, that's all that matters," she said, grudgingly.

"As long as we all feel that way, we'll get along," he said. He turned and called to Eduardo, "Let's get moving."

They mounted up and once again began to travel single file. That was just as well, Clint thought. A man involved in a conversation could always miss something, and end up dead. No amount of conversation was worth that.

● ● ●

"This is the place," Eduardo said a little over an hour later.

Clint pulled up alongside Eduardo, and Juliana hurried to join them.

"I feel evil," she said.

"It's your imagination," Clint said. "There's nothing here."

"I feel it," she said again, with feeling.

"If there was something here, the horses would feel it," he told her. The four horses were standing calmly, which meant that they weren't catching the scent of the cat.

"They feel," Clint said, "without the benefit of emotion."

"I can't help it," she said, hugging her arms. "I feel cold."

"Tell me what happened, Eduardo."

"I was not there," Eduardo said.

"Tell me what you know."

"Carlito was standing in the clearing," he said. "Alonzo said that the cat came out of a tree and knocked him down and began to maul him."

Clint looked at the clearing, which was as large as the one they had been bushwhacked by Sykes in. This one, however, had several tall trees surrounding it, and the cat could have come out of any one of them.

"I just wish I had an accurate appraisal of the size of this beast," he said, leaning his forearm on his saddle horn.

"Why does that matter?" Juliana asked. "Isn't it enough that he's deadly, a killer?"

"I like to know what I'm up against," he told her. "The two of you stay here."

"Where are you going?"

"I'm just going to ride around in the clearing," he said.

"Are you looking for tracks?"

"No," he said, "not after all this time."

"Then why—"

"We'll get things done a lot quicker if I don't have to stop and explain everything I do," he said, interrupting her. She lapsed into a resentful silence, and he started his horse forward.

He took the horse in a slow circle of the clearing, trying to figure out which way he'd go from there if he was a cat with a fresh kill behind him.

Coming back to where the two cousins waited he asked Eduardo, "Where was the cat first seen after he killed Carlito?"

"South of here," he answered, "between here and our ranch. He killed a steer a few days after."

"And then where?"

Eduardo shrugged and said, "By that time we were in the United States, looking for you."

"Juliana?" Clint asked.

"He hit a couple of the other ranches between this point, and our ranch," she said.

"What's north of here?" he asked.

"Swamps," Eduardo said. "This is home for the alligators, pumas, and the jaguars."

"But not this jaguar, eh?" Clint said, partially to himself. "This cat left the swamps and doesn't want to go back."

"Why should he?" Juliana asked. "There is less competition here for his food, and he has been very successful."

"How are the ranches laid out, Eduardo?" he asked.

"There are some to the west of here, but most of them lie to the east, and the south, like ours."

"All right," Clint said, "then let's circle to the east and work our way back south. If most of his food is in there, that's where we'll find him."

"We hope," Juliana said.

"He's not going north," Clint said, "back to the swamps. He could go west, but if the bulk of the livestock is to the east, and south, then those are our best chances."

"What if we don't find him?" she asked.

"Oh, I'm sure that if we ride around enough out here we'll find him," Clint said, then as an afterthought he added, "or he'll find us."

Chapter Thirty-Two

"I'm no hunter," Juliana said later, riding up alongside of the Gunsmith, "but shouldn't you be looking for tracks?"

"Juliana, your father got his facts a little twisted when he decided that I was a hunter," he told her. "Unless I can trip over a track, I wouldn't know it if it bit me. I was a lawman, not a big game hunter."

"Then why did he hire you?"

"Maybe he got tired of looking," he suggested. "Maybe he heard about my reputation, and figured I was the best he could do."

"If you don't kill that cat, he's going to change his mind pretty fast."

"I'll find the cat, all right," he said, "just don't be expecting me to smell him from a mile off."

At that point, they both heard Eduardo's horse begin acting up, and watched as the animal reared up on his hind legs and dumped his rider off.

"Eduardo," Juliana called, dismounting.

Clint stayed on his horse, because he felt the animal's muscles bunch beneath him.

"Easy, fella," he said.

Juliana's horse and the pack animal both began to prance about nervously.

"Is he all right?" Clint called out.

"I am fine," Eduardo assured him, climbing to his feet and dusting himself off.

"Then the two of you better grab hold of your horses," Clint told them. "These animals smell something that they don't like."

Juliana ran back and took hold of her horse's reins.

"The cat?" she asked, looking around nervously.

"I don't know," Clint said, "but it must be an animal of some kind."

Eduardo was trying to calm his horse down about twenty feet ahead of him when the animal reared and screamed. There was a flash of brown as something rushed from out of the bushes and headed straight for Eduardo. It was moving incredibly fast, but the Gunsmith's hand was faster as he drew his gun and fired at the moving target.

The animal screeched, leaped in the air once, and then fell to the ground and lay still.

"My God!" Juliana Ramirez breathed, but she wasn't looking at the dead animal, she was looking at the Gunsmith.

Clint climbed down from his horse and, keeping his gun in his hand, walked over to the dead animal and prodded it with the toe of his boot.

"A puma," he said as Eduardo and Juliana came up on either side of him. "A big one, too."

"It could have killed me," Eduardo said. He looked at Clint and said, "You saved my life."

"Probably," he said, holstering his gun. "Could this be the animal we're looking for?" he asked both of them.

"I do not think so," Eduardo said. "Alonzo said that it was definitely a jaguar that killed Carlito."

"Well, this one is certainly big enough," Clint said, "but he's no jaguar."

It was the biggest puma Clint had ever seen, and it had been torn up some in a fight not long ago.

"Look at those wounds," Clint said. "This critter was in a

fight with something bigger and stronger, and not long ago, either. He must have been half crazy from the pain, which was what made him go after you like that. Pumas are usually a little more selective about attacking their prey.''

"I've never seen anything so fast," Juliana said, as if she had just found her voice.

"Oh, he moved fast, all right," Clint said, prodding the animal again.

"No," Juliana said, "I meant you. I've never seen anyone draw a gun so fast, and you hit him with your first shot, as fast as he was moving.''

"He was a big target," Clint said, playing it down. "I couldn't have missed if I wanted to.''

"That's nonsense," she said. "I'm a good shot, and I barely had time to move. I don't think I could have got him with one shot.''

"Sure you could," he said. "You were just surprised, that's all.''

"And you weren't," she said. "That's another thing. You weren't at all surprised.''

"Yes, I was," Clint said, "but I didn't let that stop me. I wasn't about to lose my guide, not when we've got a jaguar to find.''

He turned away from the dead puma and walked back to his horse. Speaking to it in soft tones, he calmed it down. Although the puma was dead, its smell was still spooking the horses.

"Come on," he said, mounting up, "let's get these horses away from here, and then we'll talk.''

With one last look at the dead cat both Eduardo and Juliana walked back to their horses and mounted up.

They circled around the carcass and rode on for about a half a mile before Clint called out for them to stop.

"There's blood on the ground," he said, looking down.

"I thought you weren't a hunter," Juliana said. She was

looking at Clint with renewed interest and respect.

"Anybody can see blood," Clint said, dismounting. He walked around a bit, then turned and said, "That puma had some nasty wounds, but I don't think he accounted for all of this blood himself."

"Meaning what?" she asked.

"Meaning we may have a whole new problem on our hands," he said, mounting up again.

"Do you want to let us in on it?" Juliana asked.

"With all the blood that's here," he said, and even Eduardo and Juliana were able to see it, "I think that puma may have done a little damage of his own to that jaguar."

"Well," Juliana said, "at least we know the beast can bleed. No devil would do that."

"Yeah," Clint said gravely, "but we also know that this cat is wounded now, and that just makes him all the more deadly."

Chapter Thirty-Three

They camped that night in a small clearing and built an extra large fire.

"You don't expect the jaguar to attack at night, do you?" Juliana asked. "With the fire, and all?"

"Why do your people call him the Devil Cat?" Clint asked.

"Because he is not as other cats are," Eduardo said. "He has the devil inside of him."

"One of us will stay on watch at all times," Clint said. "I'll take the first watch and I'll wake Eduardo in two hours. I want to get an early start in the morning."

"Why don't you let me take the first watch?" Juliana offered.

Clint looked at her in surprise and said, "I didn't want you to accuse me of giving you all of the menial jobs."

"I'm sorry I said that," she said, lowering her eyes.

"Forget it," Clint said. "You and Eduardo better get some sleep, now. If the cat is wounded, we're going to have to be extra alert tomorrow."

"Come, Juliana," Eduardo said.

While the other two settled in to sleep Clint poured himself another cup of coffee. He avoided looking into the fire, because he did not want the flames to affect his night vision. He listened for the horses, because they would give him warning if the Devil Cat—or any cat—approached.

After about twenty minutes he heard a sound behind him and turned to find Juliana.

"Can I sit with you?"

"You should be sleeping."

She sat next to him and said, "I can't sleep."

"I think there's a little coffee left in the pot."

"No, thanks," she said. "I'm a little frightened, I think, and maybe sitting next to you for a few minutes will help."

"You're frightened?" he asked, feigning surprise.

"Hard to believe, right?" she said. "Well, ever since that puma this afternoon I've been frightened. It moved so quickly, and if it wasn't for you it would have killed—"

"But it didn't," Clint said.

"I know, but it wasn't even the jaguar and only your quickness kept Eduardo alive. What will happen when we find the cat we're seeking?"

"The same thing, hopefully," Clint said. "We'll kill it, and this will be all over."

"Will it?" she asked. "That jaguar has been doing a lot of damage, and I'm afraid some of it might be permanent."

"Like the way your father feels about Alonzo?"

She looked at him and said, "Yes. I think perhaps that you were right last night."

"About what?"

"Maybe I should take Alonzo and leave. We have money of our own, you know."

"Where would you go?"

"I don't know," she said, shrugging her shoulders. "Maybe to the United States." She looked at him and said, "Maybe we should go back with you."

He looked out into the darkness and said, "Once we kill that cat, Juliana, maybe you should give it some time before you make a decision."

"You don't want me—us—to go back with you?"

"I don't want you to do anything you're going to be sorry for," he said. "Think it over, and give your father a chance. Eduardo said that he feels as if the Devil Cat is his own personal curse. Once we remove that, maybe things will be different."

"Carlito will still be gone," she said. "That cannot be changed."

"The rest of it can, though," he said, "if you give it half a chance."

"Perhaps," she said.

"Get some sleep," he advised her. "I don't want you falling asleep in the saddle tomorrow."

"Yes," she said. She leaned over and kissed him and then said into his ear, "I wish we could be together tonight."

She got up quickly before he could reply and went back to her bedroll.

Clint got up and walked over to where the horses were picketed and made sure they were secured, then went back to the fire to put on another pot of coffee.

He was pouring himself a cup when the horses began to act up, prancing about nervously and tossing their heads.

Clint stood up, his hand hovering near his hip.

That was when he heard the cat.

Chapter Thirty-Four

The night was quiet, and the sound he heard was the rumbling in the Devil Cat's chest.

"What is it?" Juliana asked, getting to her feet. "Duardo," she hissed, touching her cousin's shoulder. He woke with a start, and got to his feet. Both cousins rushed to Clint's side.

"What is it?" she asked again.

"Shhh," he hissed at them. "He's out there."

"Where?" Juliana asked.

"Circling," Clint said, following the sound with his ears.

Eduardo rushed back to his bedroll for his rifle, and when he came back to the fire with it he lifted it to his shoulder.

"No," Clint said, knocking the barrel down towards the ground.

"I want to get him."

"He knows where we are," Clint said, still listening intently, "and we don't know where he is. It's not going to do any good to start firing shots at random."

"But—"

"Go stay by the horses, Eduardo," Clint said. "Try to keep them calm, or they may break loose, and then we'll be stuck. Okay?"

"If he comes near the horses, I will shoot him," Eduardo said.

"Fine," Clint said, "but don't fire until you can see him."

157

Eduardo nodded and moved over to where the horses were.

"What should I do?" Juliana asked.

"Get your rifle," he said, "and come back by the fire."

She obeyed, and came back holding her rifle. "Now what?"

"Just be still."

Eduardo was holding the horses now, trying to keep them quiet, and the sounds of the Devil Cat were more audible now. They could all hear him.

"He's just going around us," Juliana said.

"I know," Clint said. He was turning with the cat, keeping his back to the fire.

"Shouldn't we go and look for him?"

"In the dark?" he asked. "We'd be easy prey for him. That's what he wants, Juliana. He wants us to leave the fire and go out into the dark, where he is."

"You talk about him as if he was intelligent."

"The way he's circling us, and letting us hear him, makes me think that maybe he is."

"You think that maybe he *is* a devil cat?"

"I think that he's out there, prowling around, and that he has no intention of coming any closer."

"That suits me just fine," she said, holding on to her rifle tightly.

For the next half hour, the cat continued to circle them, growling deep in his chest, and occasionally out loud, a sound that made Juliana jump each time she heard it.

"I don't know how much more of this I can take," she said at one point.

"Just relax," he said.

"Sure," she said, "like you are."

She looked up at him, then, the way he was tensed for any move the cat might make. He reminded her of an animal himself, poised to strike.

The horse began to act up again, and Juliana looked over

at where Eduardo was standing, holding them.

Or where he had been standing.

"Clint!" she said, and the alarm in her tone made him look down at her.

"Eduardo's gone!" she said.

Clint looked over at the horses and saw that Eduardo was no longer standing with them.

"Shit," he said. "He went out there after the cat."

"We have to go after him," she said, standing up.

"No," Clint said, putting one hand on her shoulder. "We can't go out there."

"We have to," she said. "He'll be killed."

"Juliana, the cat is trying to split us up," he said, "or separate us from the horses. Our only chance is to stay together."

"But Eduardo is out there, now."

"And we're here, together, with the horses. If we go out there after him, the cat will hit the horses."

"But he's alone!"

"And if I go out there after him, you'll be alone," Clint said. "If you go out after him, I'll be alone. Any way we go, Eduardo's the one that put us all in jeopardy by going out there. By doing that he's assumed the responsibility for his own life. My responsibility is to myself, to you, and to those horses."

"I'm going out there," she said, trying to pull away from his touch.

"No," he said, tightening his hold on her, "you're not. Sit back down."

He pushed and she sat back down, reluctantly.

"All right," she said, "but if Eduardo is killed, I'll never forgive you."

"At least you'll be alive," he said, "to hate me for a long, long time."

● ● ●

They began to listen intently for some sign that Eduardo had found the cat—or that the cat had found him—but all they heard were the same sounds.

"That cat is working on our nerves," Clint said,

"What's happening out there?" Juliana asked, impatiently.

"I don't know," Clint said. "The cat has had enough time to go after Eduardo. Why wouldn't he—unless he just doesn't want to?"

"But why not?"

"I don't know," Clint said.

"But we have to wait?"

"Yes, we do," Clint said. "If he gets us all to go out there, then he'll have his pick. We've got to stay right here and wait him out."

"Wait until daylight, you mean?"

"If that's what it takes," he said. "I only hope Eduardo will come back before then. The longer he's out there, the less chance he has of getting back at all."

Chapter Thirty-Five

The situation didn't change until almost daylight, and even Clint was starting to feel the fatigue when Eduardo finally appeared.

"Duardo," Juliana cried out, rising and running to meet him.

He looked worn out and disheveled, but other than that did not seem to be wounded at all, except for some scrapes and scratches from the brush.

Juliana allowed him to lean on her and walked him back to the fire.

"I'm glad you're all right, Eduardo," Clint said.

"He seemed to be leading me on," Eduardo said, as if he hadn't heard Clint. "He always seemed to be just ahead of me."

"It was foolish of you to go out there after the cat," Clint said. "You risked all of our lives by doing it."

"I am sorry," Eduardo said, "but I just could not wait any longer."

"Clint wouldn't let me come out after you," Juliana explained, as if afraid her cousin would think she hadn't wanted to try and help him.

"No, he was right not to let you go," Eduardo said.

"Thank you," Clint said.

"What do we do now?" Eduardo asked.

Clint looked at the sky. "It's almost daylight. I get the

feeling that cat has accomplished what he set out to accomplish."

"What's that?" Juliana asked.

"He kept us up all night," Clint explained.

"How could an animal be that smart?" she asked. "It's not possible."

"He is a devil," Eduardo said.

Clint lifted his head up and listened, but there were no longer any sounds to indicate that the cat was still out there.

"He's gone," Clint said. "He got what he came for, and now he's gone."

"What are we supposed to do now?" Juliana asked.

"Let's mount up and get away from here," Clint said. "Maybe we'll do what you were asking me about all along, Juliana."

"What?"

"Tracks," he said, "we'll look for tracks. He was all around us last night. We should be able to find some tracks to indicate which way he went. When we do, we'll get on his trail. Get that fire out, Eduardo."

They broke camp, saddled their horses and mounted up.

"Let's just circle the camp the way he did for a while and check out the ground. There must be some indication of which way he went."

They rode around in a circle twice, with Clint getting down every so often to check out the ground.

"There are tracks over tracks, here," he said, "but they don't seem to lead anywhere. They just go in circles."

"But he's not anywhere around here," Juliana said. "There must be some tracks showing which way he went."

"Perhaps we just cannot see them," Eduardo proposed.

"If we can see these we should be able to see others," Clint said, "unless . . ."

"Unless what?"

He looked up at them and said, "Unless we're only seeing what he wants us to see."

Juliana shook her head and said, "No animal can be that smart."

"A devil," Eduardo said in a low voice, and both Juliana and Clint looked at him.

I'd hate to think you were right, Clint said to himself. "Let's get out of here," he said aloud, mounting up.

They kept to their original plan of riding east and south, and Clint was annoyed with himself for what he was thinking.

The cat couldn't be a devil, that was just not acceptable, but how could he be so intelligent? How could he do something like he did last night, circling the camp and keeping them awake like that? Or were they just giving the animal too much credit?

"What are you thinking?" Juliana asked.

"The same thing we're all thinking," he said. "What kind of creature are we dealing with here? I would have thought that a wounded animal couldn't act the way he did last night. A wounded animal wouldn't—or shouldn't—have that much patience."

"Then perhaps Eduardo and everyone else is right," she said. "Maybe he does have the devil in him."

"I can't believe that," Clint said, but he wasn't as sure as he once was. "Not yet, anyway."

By noon Clint had already had to prod both Juliana and Eduardo twice each to keep them awake, and was himself starting to feel as if he would fall asleep in the saddle.

"I think we had better stop for a while," he finally said, calling them to a halt.

"But we have to catch him," Eduardo said. "How far away can he be?"

"I don't know," Clint said, "but the only thing we've got to catch right now, Eduardo, is some sleep. One of us is going to have to stand watch while the other two get some sleep."

"I'll stand watch," Eduardo said, although he looked as if he were already half asleep.

"Why you?"

"Because you are the hunter," Eduardo said, "and because Juliana is right, she is a better shot than I am."

"You're the guide," Clint reminded him.

"We all know I have not done much guiding, Clint," Eduardo said. "We are simply riding around, waiting for the jaguar to decide to face us. When he does, I think that you and Juliana should have steady hands, and clear eyes."

Clint studied the young man, and then said, "Eduardo, you continue to amaze me. You have the watch."

Chapter Thirty-Six

They found a formation of rocks which they were able to camp against, so that they would not have to sit out in the open, leaving themselves vulnerable and making it difficult for Eduardo to be on the lookout.

"Two hours ought to be enough, Eduardo," Clint said. "We just need to take the edge off this exhaustion."

"I understand," Eduardo said. "You can count on me."

"Can we count on you not to do anything foolish again?" Clint asked.

Eduardo looked sheepish. "You can. I have learned my lesson."

"Good."

They didn't bother to unsaddle the horses. Clint and Juliana simply lay down on the ground with their heads cradled in their arms, and fell asleep.

It was all Eduardo could do to keep awake. He kept drifting off, his eyes going out of focus, and he'd have to shake his head to straighten himself out again. The last thing he wanted to do was fall asleep and endanger all of their lives again, as he had done the night before.

Going out into the dark after the devil cat had been quite an experience for him. First of all, although he admitted his foolishness, he was surprised that he'd had the courage to be that foolish.

Once he was in the dark, he thought that he was hunting the

cat, but it soon became apparent to him that this was not the case. Although he had the gun, it was the cat that was hunting him—or so he thought. As it turned out, the cat had simply led him about, as if he were a horse and the beast was holding the reins. At one point, Eduardo wanted to break it off and go back into camp, but he had been unable to. He had not realized it then, but now he was certain he had been in some sort of trance: the Devil Cat had used his evil powers to entrance him and keep him out there until almost daylight. As the sky had begun to lighten, it was as if he had awakened from sleepwalking. He had not even been sure how much time had gone by. When he went back into camp he had been afraid to explain any of this to Clint or Juliana, for fear that they would think him mad.

As he sat now, standing watch, drifting off now and then, he convinced himself that the cat was out there somewhere, watching him, once again trying to use his evil powers to put Eduardo under his spell.

It would not happen again, he swore to himself. He needed some way to make sure that he stayed awake and alert. He searched the ground and his eyes fell upon a sharp stone. He picked it up and fit it into his palm, with the point digging into his flesh. When he closed his hand over it and squeezed, the point pierced his flesh, drawing blood. Every time he felt himself drifting off, he would squeeze his hand, and the pain would keep him awake.

The Devil Cat would not enter his mind and use him as a tool against his cousin, and Clint.

When almost two hours had passed Eduardo, despite the pain in his hand, started to feel hungry. There was some beef jerky in his saddlebag, so he rose and walked over to his horse. Leaning his rifle against a rock he stuck his uninjured hand into the saddlebag for the beef jerky . . . and that was when he saw the Devil Cat.

Chapter Thirty-Seven

The beast was standing about twenty feet away from him, out in the open, staring at him.

Standing with his hand in the saddlebag, and his rifle on the ground, Eduardo's mouth went dry with fear, and a chill ran up his back. Slowly, he opened his other hand and allowed the bloody stone to fall to the ground.

The cat simply stood there, staring at him, and he felt compelled to look at the animal's eyes. They remained like that for seemingly endless minutes, and suddenly Eduardo felt as if he could not breathe. He became convinced that the Devil Cat was trying to possess him, and he had to find the will to resist. His will was the only thing that stood between life and death for him, his cousin and Clint.

The cat's eyes seemed to glow, and heat seemed to be emanating from them. Sweat broke out on Eduardo's brow, and he could feel it dripping down his back, as well. He opened his mouth to call out to Clint, but no sound would come out.

The beast had struck him dumb . . . or was it simply fear that had accomplished that?

As he could not speak, neither could he move. They were easy prey for the cat as things stood, yet why did he not approach?

Staring at the animal, Eduardo had to admit that the beast was beautiful, but that only served to make it even more evil.

Eduardo found himself doing something he had not done for many years.

He began to pray to God, asking for some kind of miracle. *Give me the will, and the courage, to move,* he asked. *Just let me shout and warn others, even if my life should be forfeit.*

Suddenly, the sweat had built up to such an extent on his brow that several drops fell into his eyes. Stung by the salt from his own perspiration, Eduardo reflexively closed his eyes . . . and was free!

He kept his eyes closed, even though terror made him want to open them again. He could not see the cat at all now. Was the beast advancing on them, ready to tear them to pieces?

He had to do something and do it now, before it was too late for all of them.

His muscles tensed and then he opened his eyes, shouted, "No!" and sprang for his rifle.

His hands closed on the gun and he fell to the ground, rolled over, and came up pointing the rifle at the cat . . . only the animal was gone!

"Eduardo!" Clint shouted.

Eduardo's own shout had awakened Clint and Juliana, but all they saw was the man on his knees, pointing his rifle at nothing.

"Eduardo, what is it?" Juliana asked, running to his side.

Clint noticed that Eduardo's shirt was drenched with perspiration, and that the man's hands were shaking as he held his rifle tightly. There was a smear of blood on the gun, coming from his left hand.

"Eduardo," Clint said, placing his hand on the barrel of the rifle.

"He was here," Eduardo said.

"Who?" Juliana asked. "The Devil Cat?"

Her cousin nodded and said, "He was here, trying to possess me."

Clint and Juliana exchanged glances, and Juliana put her

arm around her cousin's shoulders.

"Eduardo," she said, softly, "maybe you fell asleep and dreamed that the cat—"

"I did not fall asleep!" Eduardo said, vehemently. "I would not do that. See?" he added, showing them his bloody left hand. "I used pain to make sure I did not fall asleep."

Juliana gasped, took off her neckerchief and used it to wrap Eduardo's hand.

"He was standing right there, looking at me," Eduardo said, "and I couldn't move. I couldn't move and I couldn't speak and I could not take my eyes off of him. He was trying to possess me, but I would not allow it!"

"All right, Eduardo," Clint said, softly. "Lower the rifle and I'll go and see."

Reluctantly, Eduardo allowed Clint to push the barrel of the rifle down so that it was pointing towards the ground.

Clint walked over to where Eduardo said the cat was, and was not sure what he expected to find, but sure enough, there were the cat's tracks, big as life, and seemingly fresh.

He walked back to where Juliana crouched with her arm still around Eduardo and said, "He's right. The cat was here."

"Oh, my God," Juliana breathed.

"Come on, Eduardo," Clint said, helping him to his feet. "We've got to get mounted up and see if we can catch up to him."

"We will catch up to him," Eduardo said, "when he wants us to. He is playing with us."

"Well, he didn't get us this time, thanks to you," Clint said. "Now let's go and get him."

Eduardo looked at Clint, and Clint could see the naked terror in the man's eyes. He knew that if he could not get Eduardo to mount his horse, the terror would never leave him.

"Let's get him, Eduardo," he said, softly but firmly.

Slowly, Eduardo's eyes seemed to focus on the Gunsmith's face, and then the young man simply said, "Yes," and Clint knew that he'd be all right—for now.

They mounted up and started after the cat.

For some reason, the beast's tracks were suddenly quite clear and very easy to follow. Clint thought again about what Eduardo had said, but could not convince himself that the cat was simply allowing them to see his tracks now, in order to lead them to some predetermined place.

He would not allow himself to think such a thing.

Each step their horses took seemed to be taking them closer and closer to the Ramirez ranch, and Clint wondered if the cat was headed there, for some reason.

Was he somehow drawn towards the Ramirez ranch? *Was* he Raphael Ramirez's own personal curse?

Clint suddenly had the strange feeling—or a premonition—that before nightfall, this whole matter would be resolved, one way or another.

He could not, however, have imagined how.

Chapter Thirty-Eight

"Slow down," Clint said, holding up his hand.

"What's wrong?" Juliana asked.

"I don't know," Clint said. His lawman's sixth sense was at work, even though he had not been a lawman for some time now. "Something's not right."

"Is it the cat?"

"I can't say," he replied.

That was when he heard the shot, and the sound the bullet made when it smacked into Eduardo's flesh, throwing him from his horse as if he had been yanked by a rope.

"Duardo!" Juliana shouted.

"Dismount!" Clint shouted. "I'll get Eduardo!"

Unlike the first place they had been bushwhacked, this one offered plenty of cover. He jumped from his horse, taking his rifle with him, grabbed Eduardo and dragged him behind a large cluster of rocks.

"Juliana," he called out.

"Here," she replied. She had found cover behind the trunk of a large, fallen tree. "How is Eduardo?"

Clint took a quick look at the wound, which was on the right side of his lower back. He couldn't tell how bad the wound was. For all he knew, the bullet could have also struck a lung.

"He's all right, for now," Clint replied.

"Eduardo," he said.

"Yes?" Eduardo answered, and his voice reflected the amount of pain he was feeling.

"Just try and hold on," Clint said. "We'll get out of here." Clint took out the New Line Colt and handed it to Eduardo. "Hold onto that."

Eduardo nodded, and his hand closed over the little weapon.

Clint stuck his head up, and two more shots were fired. They both bounced off the rocks near his face.

They were surrounded by rocks and brush, and whoever was doing the shooting could be anywhere. It was not as easy to pick out their cover as it had been the first time . . . and Clint was sure that they were dealing with the same person they'd dealt with the first time. Who else had cause to bushwhack them?

"Sykes," he called. "I know that's you, Sykes."

There was a moment's silence, and then Sykes's voice answered. "Yeah, it's me, Adams, and I got some good boys with me this time. I'm paying them out of my own pocket, which will give you some idea of how important this is to me."

"What is it?" Clint asked. "The money, Sykes? Is that what you want?"

"It's more than that now, Adams," Sykes replied. "I want you, now."

"Then let the others go."

"No way," Sykes said. "If they're with you, they're gonna die with you."

Clint decided to try a new tactic.

"Sykes, listen to me," he called. "There's a jaguar loose around here, one that they call the Devil Cat. We've been hunting him. You not only have to deal with us, you've got to deal with him, too."

"Crap!" Sykes called out. "Ain't no cat in the world

wants to be this close to where there's so many people. If you were hunting a cat, he's long gone, now.''

"This is not a normal cat, Sykes.''

"Keep trying, Adams,'' Sykes said, "but you ain't gonna talk your way out of here. My men are spreading out, and in a few seconds they'll be all around you. You're gonna be eating lead from every angle, and there ain't nothing you can do about it.''

"What about you and me, Sykes?'' Clint called. "If it's me you want, then let's step out into the open and do it right, do it fair.''

Sykes laughed at him. "I ain't never claimed to be a fair man, Adams. I do things my way. You only got a few seconds, Adams. You and your friends better make your peace.''

Sykes fell silent then, and Clint was out of ideas.

"Clint, what do we do?'' Juliana called.

He didn't have an answer for her.

"Eduardo, I've got to go over by Juliana,'' he said to the wounded man.

His face etched with pain, Eduardo merely waved his hand weakly, telling him to go.

Clint got up into a crouch, then broke into a run towards Juliana, drawing no fire.

"Move around all you want, Adams,'' Sykes called. "This time it's all over.''

When Clint reached Juliana her face was drawn, and her knuckles were white as she gripped her rifle. She'd been smart enough to take her weapon when she dismounted.

"I told you not to come,'' Clint said to her. "Maybe next time you'll listen to me.''

The humor was lost on her.

"What do we do now?'' she asked again. "Who is that man?''

"His name is Sykes,'' Clint said. "Eduardo won some

money from him in Santa Ruiz and I stopped him when he tried to take it back.''

"Give him the money, then."

"You heard him, Juliana. It's more than the money, now.''

"Then we are dead.''

"Not yet," Clint said. "We can't just sit here and wait for his men to get into position.''

"We don't even know how many men he's got," she pointed out.

"Good point," he said. "He could very well be all alone. All the more reason why I've got to go out in the brush and move around. I might be able to do some damage.''

"What about us?''

He touched her arm and said, "Honey, all I can tell you is stay low, and pray. With a little luck, we'll get out of this.''

He'd lied to her. They were going to need a hell of a lot of luck.

Sykes was feeling very satisfied with himself. He had rounded up four men who would slit their own mothers' throats for a dollar and had offered them considerably more than that to help him kill Clint Adams. These boys wouldn't run at the first sign of a fight, no sir. These were hardcases who would take it personal if Adams tried to fight back. It'd be like he was taking the money right out of their pockets.

It had taken he and his men some time to track Adams and the others down, but finding out the names of the people Adams had been with in Santa Ruiz had been a big help. Ramirez had one of the biggest ranches in Paraguay, and it hadn't been hard to find. From there the rest was easy.

Actually, what had happened was that Sykes and his men had accidentally run across Clint, Eduardo and Juliana's trail while heading for the ranch and followed it until they caught up to them. Sykes, however, would not admit such a thing to his men and as tough as the men were, none of them would consider calling Sykes a liar to his face. That wouldn't be the healthy thing to do. And besides, he was paying them each a lot of money. It had been a long time since any of these men had seen a hundred dollars in one place.

Sykes made himself comfortable, waiting for the signal that his men were in position. This time, he thought, this time it was going to end differently.

He had no idea just how right he would be.

Chapter Thirty-Nine

Clint hated to leave his rifle behind, but it would be easier for him to move through the brush noiselessly without it. Besides, as long as he had his modified Colt, he was sure he could handle almost any situation that came along.

"Here, take this," he said.

"What—"

"Juliana, listen to me," he said. "I have to go into the brush and move around, and Eduardo is hurt. That leaves just you. If any shooting starts, you're going to have to fire back. Can you do that?"

"I have to, don't I?" she asked. "I don't have much of a choice."

"No, you don't," Clint agreed. "Not if we're going to have any chance of getting out of here alive."

"Do you really think we have a chance?" she asked.

"We've always got a chance," he said. He leaned over to kiss her, and then added, "Stay here. Don't try to get over to Eduardo because there's nothing you can do for him here."

"Is he going to die?"

"First things first, Juliana," he said, squeezing her arm. "Let's concentrate on getting us out of here."

She nodded, and he melted into the brush.

Gun in hand he crouched in the brush, listening for the sounds men would make moving through it. Still, even if he heard sounds, how could he be sure it was Sykes's men, and not the cat?

He listened intently for several minutes, and satisfied himself that he could hear no one moving about. Either Sykes's men were very quiet, or he had lied about them and was alone. Clint began to move himself, hoping to circle around to the other side of the clearing, where he hoped Sykes was hiding.

He had moved only a few yards when he tripped over something. Only his excellent reflexes kept him from accidentally squeezing the trigger on his gun, giving himself away.

He stumbled to one knee, and when he turned, he saw what he had tripped over.

It was a man, and his throat had been torn out.

Clint stared at the ghastly, open wound, and knew that the Devil Cat had done it—but when? Was this one of Sykes's men or someone else? How long had this body been here?

The wound was still bleeding, so the kill was recent. It must have been one of Sykes's men, but how could the cat have killed him so quietly, with neither man nor beast making a sound?

Clint got up and continued on through the brush. If Sykes had one man, then he might very well have had more, even though they couldn't be heard. He moved even more carefully than before, because not only might there be more men, but there was evidence that the cat was near, as well.

Clint walked several more yards, and almost stumbled over another body. Now totally confused, he stopped and stared at the dead man. As with the other, this one's throat had been torn out, and he hadn't made a sound.

This was impossible!

How could a cat attack a man and tear his throat out—no, two men . . . and who was to say it was only two?

Sykes had to be waiting for his men to get into position, and would be wondering why they hadn't signaled him by now. That would hold up any rush Sykes might make on Juliana and Eduardo's position. Clint decided he'd look around further, this time specifically looking for Sykes's other men—dead.

He found them.

They were lying yards apart, and had been killed the same way as the other two. He looked further, but didn't find any others. He went back to where the last man was and sat down by the body.

Four men, all killed the same way, and all dying silently. Horribly mangled, but dying in silence.

How? And why?

And did this mean that Sykes was now alone?

Sykes was alone.

At least, he felt like he was alone. None of his men had signaled their position yet, and that didn't make sense.

What the hell is going on here, he thought, angrily.

It was supposed to be different, this time. Where were his men?

He stood up, then, and decided to hell with them. He didn't need them. He'd do it himself.

"Adams!" he called out. "Adams! Let's make it just me and you, Adams!"

He'd kill him man to man, and then he'd take care of those cowards he hired.

Chapter Forty

Clint was working his way back through the brush towards Juliana when he heard Sykes call out.

"Clint," she hissed in surprise when he appeared behind her.

"Easy."

"What happened?"

"I'm not sure," he said, "but all of Sykes's men are dead."

"You killed them?"

"I didn't have to," he said. "They were all killed by the cat."

"What?" she asked. "But we didn't hear—"

"I know we didn't."

"Come on, Adams!" Sykes called.

"What does he want?" she asked.

"He's probably wondering what happened to his men," Clint said. "Maybe he's decided to go ahead without them."

"Step out, Adams!"

"What about your men, Sykes?" Clint called. "Where are they?"

"They won't interfere," Sykes called back.

"No, they won't," Clint called back. "They're all dead, Sykes."

There was silence, and then Sykes called out, "What are you talking about?"

"Your men were killed by the big cat I told you about," Clint told him.

"That's impossible," Sykes said. "We would have heard."

"We should have," Clint said, "but we didn't. I found the bodies."

"You're lying!"

"How else would I know that there were four other men, aside from yourself," Clint said. He recalled something about the fourth man and added, "and that one of them had a scar on his forehead."

Clint listened for Sykes's answer, but one never came.

How? Sykes's mind screamed. *How did he know that? Had he killed the four of them himself? And if so, why blame it on some big cat?*

He was about to answer Clint Adams, to call him out, when he heard a sound behind him. He turned, saw the jaguar and opened his mouth to scream as the animal silently leaped at him. . . .

"Why doesn't he answer?" Juliana asked.

"I don't know," Clint said.

"Maybe he's gone," she said, hopefully.

"There's only one way to find out," Clint said, standing up.

"Clint," she said, "if he's still there he'll kill you. Stay down."

"It'll be all right, Juliana," he said.

He started across the clearing, and Juliana stood up and followed him. As he crossed, he gradually increased his pace, because he thought he knew what he'd find.

As he reached the other side and broke through the brush he found Sykes's body.

His throat was gone, just like the others, and he had died without making a sound.

Chapter Forty-One

"Oh, my God!" Juliana said.

Clint turned and took her by the shoulders.

"Come on, Juliana," he said, "you don't want to see that."

"But what happened?" she asked.

"He was killed by the cat, just like the others," he explained.

"But we didn't hear anything."

"I know," he said. "I can't explain it, and what's more, I'm not going to try. Let's see about Eduardo."

They went back across the clearing to where he had left Eduardo and found him still conscious, but glassy-eyed.

"What happened?"

"It's all over," Clint said. "Sykes and his men are dead."

"Killed by the cat," Juliana said, as she applied pressure and a piece of her shirt as a bandage to his wound.

"He's lost a lot of blood," she said. "We've got to get him back to the ranch."

"And we will, as soon as I round up the horses."

"We cannot go back until we have killed the Devil Cat," Eduardo argued.

"We'll have to see about that another time, Eduardo," Clint said. "Besides, I'm not so sure we ought to keep calling it the Devil Cat."

"Why not?" Juliana asked.

"Well, whether we like it or not, that animal saved our bacon today. I'll get the horses."

While Clint was off rounding up the horses, Juliana helped Eduardo to his feet. He was unsteady, but with her aid he stood straight enough.

"How do you feel?"

"Weak," Eduardo said, "and angry. I wanted to find the Devil Cat."

"We'll find him," she assured him, "after we get you proper medical attention."

"I suppose both Ernesto and I are lucky that Sykes was not a better shot," Eduardo said.

Clint found the horses nearby, including the packhorse, with all the supplies in tact. Why would the cat go after four men when nearby there were four easier prey to down?

He gathered up the reins of the four horses and led them back to where he left Juliana and Eduardo.

Even though he was as alert as ever, he did not hear the jaguar, which was walking right behind them. Later, he would wonder what kind of animal could disguise his scent so that the horses did not react to it.

Juliana and Eduardo looked up as Clint reentered the clearing, leading all four horses.

"He found them," Juliana said, with relief. "We'll have you back at the ranch very shortly."

Eduardo nodded, and then his eyes widened as he saw the jaguar enter the clearing behind Clint.

It began to circle to its left, so that the horses were not between it and Clint, and then it sprang forward.

"No," Eduardo shouted. He raised the Colt New Line and began pulling the trigger.

Clint turned as the animal screamed in pain. Eduardo fired

all six shots, and at least two found their mark, but the bullets were too small to do anything but slow him down and throw off his leap.

He was in the air as Clint drew his gun and in a split second Clint realized that this was the largest cat he had ever seen.

As it went by him one paw struck Clint high on the right shoulder, the claw raking him. His right arm went numb, and his gun fell from his hand.

The jaguar landed, and then turned to face him again, bleeding from two small wounds.

"Shoot, Juliana, shoot," Eduardo said. "It's up to you."

Juliana raised the rifle to her shoulder and barely had time to sight down the barrel before the jaguar crouched, and then sprang.

She fired once and the bullet struck the cat, though it was not a killing shot. The jaguar's leap fell short, and it struck the ground unsteadily.

Clint, seeing his chance, sprang for his gun, picked it up and turned to face the cat.

The jaguar staggered, but drew his haunches in for a final leap. When it came, Clint fired into the Devil Cat's chest. The cat flipped in mid leap, and fell on its back, dead.

Clint was staring down at the dead animal when Juliana helped Eduardo walk over next to him, so they could all look down at the feared Devil Cat.

"That was it," Clint said.

"You got him," Eduardo said.

"*We* got him," Clint said. "It took the three of us."

"Are you all right?" Juliana asked.

Clint holstered his gun left-handed and then probed the claw marks on his upper right arm.

"I've had worse," he said. He stared down at the cat and then shook his head.

"What's wrong?" Juliana asked.

"I just can't believe it's dead," he said. "This animal killed five men without making a sound, without letting them make a sound. He followed me into this clearing without my hearing him and without spooking the horses. You would have thought that it would take more than bullets to kill him."

"You mean you really started to think that he was a Devil Cat?" Juliana asked.

Clint looked at both Eduardo and Juliana, who were looking at him expectantly, and then said, "I think we'd better get back to the ranch, let your uncle know that his own personal curse has ended, and get Eduardo and me cleaned up."

"You mean you *didn't* start to believe in the Devil Cat?" she asked.

Clint looked down at the massive jaguar, prodded it with his foot, and then said, "Hell, it was just a big cat."

GREAT BOOKS

E-BOOKS

AUDIOBOOKS

& MORE

Visit us today

www.speakingvolumes.us